Elizabeth fol ... "Amy, I want to talk to you."

"I don't have time right now, Elizabeth," Amy answered uneasily. "Some kids are waiting for me."

"Some Unicorns, you mean." Elizabeth's blue-green eyes were flashing.

"Well, what about it?" Amy shot back. "What's wrong with the Unicorns? Just because they don't happen to like you very much—"

"I don't care whether the Unicorns like me or not," Elizabeth retorted icily. "But I do have a right to get upset when I hear that they're spreading stories about me. A story that they could have only heard from you."

"It was the truth. I have a right to tell the truth, don't I?" Amy asked.

"Not when you're telling it just to hurt somebody," Elizabeth said angrily. And since when did you start worrying about the truth? That stuff you've been telling the Unicorns about the fire—you know it's all a lie!"

"That's enough, Elizabeth," Amy shouted. "I don't have to stand here and listen to this one minute longer!"

The SWEET VALLEY TWINS series, published by Bantam Books.
Ask your bookseller for any titles you have missed.

SWEET VALLEY TWINS SUPER CHILLERS

SWEET VALLEY TWINS SUPER EDITIONS

SWEET VALLEY TWINS

Amy Moves In

Written by
Jamie Suzanne

Created by
FRANCINE PASCAL

A BANTAM BOOK
NEW YORK · TORONTO · LONDON · SYDNEY · AUCKLAND

AMY MOVES IN

A BANTAM BOOK 0 553 40188 2

Originally published in U.S.A. by Bantam Skylark Books

First publication in Great Britain

PRINTING HISTORY
Bantam edition published 1991
Reprinted 1991
Sweet Valley High ® and Sweet Valley Twins are registered
trademarks of Francine Pascal.

Conceived by Francine Pascal.

Produced by Daniel Weiss Associates, Inc., 33 West 17th Street,
New York, NY 10011

Bantam Books are published by Transworld Publishers Ltd.,
61–63 Uxbridge Road, Ealing, London W5 5SA,
in Australia by Transworld Publishers (Australia) Pty. Ltd.,
15–23 Helles Avenue, Moorebank, NSW 2170, and in New
Zealand by Transworld Publishers (N.Z.) Ltd., Cnr. Moselle
and Waipareira Avenues, Henderson, Auckland.

Made and printed in Great Britain by
BPCC Hazell Books
Aylesbury, Bucks, England
Member of BPCC Ltd.

Dedicated to Lisa Lande

One

Amy Sutton pushed her blond hair out of her eyes and stretched. "I think we're almost done," she said tiredly.

Elizabeth Wakefield sat back on her heels and looked at the large chart of endangered species that was spread out on the floor of the Suttons' family room. Almost two weeks ago, Ms. Caxton had assigned an important science project, and Elizabeth was pleased when she and her best friend, Amy, were teamed up. The two of them had spent practically every spare moment working on their project. And Amy was right; they didn't have much more to do. They would be ready to hand in their project right on time Monday morning.

"You're right, Amy, it's nearly finished," Eliz-

1

abeth agreed. "But we wanted to include an African elephant, remember?" She picked up a magazine and began to flip through it. "I know that I saw a picture we could use."

Amy looked carefully at the chart. "Right. And let's not forget about the rhino." Suddenly, Amy shivered a little. "Are you cold, Elizabeth? Dad has set everything we need to start a fire in the fireplace, and Mom said that we could light it as long as we were careful."

"OK," Elizabeth said absently as Amy walked over to the fireplace. She carefully cut out the picture of the elephant, and when Amy rejoined her after a few minutes, they discussed its placement on the chart. Finally, the two girls wrote a paragraph about the African elephant for their accompanying report. When it was written, Elizabeth typed the paragraph on her portable electric typewriter and Amy clipped it to the other pages of the report.

"I think that our project will be the best," Amy said with satisfaction as she put the neatly typed pages into a folder. "Anyway, I'll bet that we've put in more work than any of the other kids. We've spent hours and *hours* on this project."

Elizabeth smiled. "I know. But it hasn't really seemed like work. At least, not to me. I guess that's because we've been working together. Being together makes anything seem more like fun than like work."

"I know what you mean," Amy said with a laugh. "When you're around, I feel as if I have a real sister. You're really lucky, Elizabeth. Not only do you have a sister, but she's a *twin* sister!"

Elizabeth didn't need Amy to tell her how lucky she was. She and her twin sister, Jessica, were close, loyal friends, as well as sisters. They had the same blue-green eyes, identical dimples in their left cheeks, and the same long, silky blond hair. Elizabeth and Jessica looked so much alike that they could fool almost everybody when they wanted to, but there were big differences in their personalities.

"Having a twin is great," Elizabeth said. "But there are lots of things that I can do with you that I can't do with Jess. Like this project, for instance. Jessica would be pretty bored with it." Jessica was the kind of person who lived for the moment. Anything that took longer seemed to her to be a waste of time or much too tedious.

Amy grinned. "You're right. I can't imagine Jessica getting very excited over endangered species. Unless, of course, the species happened to be *unicorns.*"

Elizabeth laughed. Jessica was a member of the Unicorn Club, an exclusive group of the prettiest and most popular girls at Sweet Valley Middle School. The members called themselves the Unicorns because they believed that they were as beautiful and special as the mythical creatures. Every day, each member tried to wear something purple, the color of royalty, as a symbol of her importance. Elizabeth had been invited to join the club at about the same time that Jessica had joined. But after she had attended a few meetings, Elizabeth had decided that there were more important things to do than sit around chattering about boys, the latest fashions, and rock stars.

"The Snob Squad," Amy added with a giggle, reminding them of Elizabeth's nickname for the club. Amy didn't like the Unicorns either, and with good reason. Lila Fowler and Ellen Riteman had tried their best to keep Amy out of the Boosters, the cheerleading squad that the Unicorns had organized. But Amy was such an expert baton-twirler that they had to let her in, even though they had grumbled and fought hard against her. More recently, the Unicorns had tried to play a nasty trick on Amy's pen pal, Samantha Williams. If Elizabeth hadn't rescued Sam, she might have been humiliated in front of a lot of people.

Elizabeth grinned back at her friend. Sometimes it seemed as if she and Amy shared more than she and Jessica did. Neither of them thought much of the Unicorns, or of stuck-up people in general. They both enjoyed writing for the class newspaper, *The Sweet Valley Sixers*, that Elizabeth had helped to start. They were equally good students and shared a strong interest in the study of animals. Making the chart and writing the report on endangered species had been like an adventure. They weren't even nervous about handing in the project the next day, or about taking Ms. Caxton's oral quiz.

"Hey, Elizabeth," Amy said excitedly. "Why don't you stay here tonight? We can put the finishing touches on the chart after we eat dinner. And after that, we can look over our report and study for the quiz."

"Great idea," Elizabeth replied enthusiastically, jumping up from the floor. "I'll call Mom and ask."

Elizabeth dialed the number and waited for someone to answer. "Hi, Mom. I'm at Amy's. We've been working on our science project and she invited me to spend the night."

"Oh, I'm sorry, Elizabeth," Mrs. Wakefield said. "You'll have to tell Amy no. Everyone's been so busy lately that we haven't spent much time together as a family. Your father and I thought it would be nice for all five of us to have a special treat—an early dinner at the Beach View Inn. I was about to call and ask you to come home."

"OK, Mom. I'll be home soon." Elizabeth replaced the receiver with a frown. She had really wanted to stay at Amy's. But she had to agree with her mother that for the past few weeks the family hadn't been spending much time together. Mr. Wakefield had been very busy with an important case for his law firm. Mrs. Wakefield had just finished a big decorating project for Henry Dennis, the famous Hollywood scriptwriter who had recently moved to Sweet Valley. Elizabeth's brother Steven, who was on the Sweet Valley High junior varsity basketball team, seemed to be spending more and more of his after-school hours at practice. Jessica was always involved with the Unicorns, and Elizabeth had been working on her science project as well as on the *Sixers*. She could understand why her mother wanted the family to spend an evening together.

"I'm sorry, Amy," Elizabeth said regretfully. "I can't stay for dinner. My mom and dad are taking us out to eat."

"That's OK," Amy replied. "I can finish up our project. All I have to do is find a picture of a rhino. We've already got that part written, haven't we?"

Elizabeth nodded as she packed up her typewriter. "Can you bring the chart to school tomorrow?" she asked. "Or should I stop by and help you carry it?"

"Mom can drive me," Amy said. "Why don't I meet you at your locker before homeroom?"

"That would be great." When she got to the front door, Elizabeth turned and waved. "See you first thing in the morning."

*   *   *

Jessica was in her bedroom, getting ready to go to dinner. She had decided to wear a turquoise top with a short white skirt. She was sitting in front of her mirror, putting curls into her long blond hair, when Elizabeth came into the room.

"Hi, Jessica," Elizabeth said cheerily. "I wanted to see what you're wearing for dinner tonight."

Jessica put down the curling iron and turned around. "Well, it's about time you decided to come home, Elizabeth." Jessica was feeling cross. Lila had gone to Los Angeles with her father for the weekend and Ellen had spent the weekend in bed with a cold. Jessica had had nothing to do and nobody to talk to for two whole days. It had been a *very* boring weekend.

Elizabeth stared at her twin. "I was at Amy's," she explained. "We were working on our science project together."

"I know," Jessica said impatiently. "You've been working on it *forever*. When is it going to be finished?"

"We have to turn it in tomorrow," Elizabeth said.

"Well, good," Jessica replied. "Since you and Amy started working on that silly project, I've hardly seen you."

"And I've hardly seen *you*. You're usually busy with the Unicorns," Elizabeth pointed out reasonably. "And with Aaron Dallas," she added with a grin.

Jessica and Aaron had gotten together at a bowling party a few weeks ago—the same party at which Elizabeth and Todd Wilkins had gotten together. Since then, Jessica had talked practically nonstop about Aaron. Elizabeth liked Todd a lot, too, but she had plenty of other things on her mind.

"Sure, I've been busy. But I haven't been away every evening for the last two weeks, the way you have," Jessica retorted. "In fact, I've been home all weekend by myself. I had some important things I wanted to talk to you about, but you were at Amy's *all day*."

"Well, I'm here now," Elizabeth said mildly, sitting down on the bed. "What was it that was so important?"

Jessica frowned. "It wasn't that I had anything *special* to talk about. It was more that . . . well, you just don't seem to have time for me anymore."

Elizabeth looked surprised. "Jess, if I didn't know better, I'd think you were jealous."

Jessica picked up the curling iron and turned back to the mirror again. "Jealous? Give me a break. It's just that I had plenty of free time this weekend and I wanted to spend it with you."

Elizabeth grinned. The real truth was finally out. Her twin had been bored. "Well, we'll have plenty of time to talk tonight, Jessica," she said.

"But right now, I'd better get ready for dinner. And I have to call Amy. I just remembered something else we wanted to put on our chart, and I'd better remind her."

"There you go again," Jessica said, pulling a brush through her hair. "It's Amy, Amy, Amy all the time. You don't ever want to talk to *me*."

"But Amy and I are best friends," Elizabeth protested. "And we've *got* to finish our science project."

Even so, Elizabeth couldn't help but feel that there was some truth in what Jessica was saying. She *had* been spending a lot of time with Amy lately, and she probably *had* been neglecting her sister. She knew that once the Unicorns were available again, Jessica would forget all about her. Still, the last thing she wanted was for Jessica to get her feelings hurt, especially over Amy.

Elizabeth went over to her twin and gave her a big hug. "Don't worry, Jess. As soon as Amy and I hand in our science project and take our quiz, I'll spend lots of time with you."

"Promise?" Jessica asked.

"Promise," Elizabeth replied. She really meant it.

The next morning, Elizabeth arrived at school a few minutes early so that she could meet Amy by her locker, as they had agreed to do. Elizabeth waited for a long time but Amy never showed up.

Elizabeth decided that she couldn't wait any longer. *Maybe Amy forgot our plan and went straight to homeroom*, she thought.

But when Elizabeth got to homeroom, Amy's desk was empty. As she slipped into her seat, she noticed that everyone in the class was talking, in spite of the fact that the homeroom bell was ringing. The room seemed charged with excitement.

Olivia Davidson leaned across the aisle. "Hi, Elizabeth," she said eagerly. "Do you know what—?"

But at that moment, Mr. Davis rapped on his desk for order, and Elizabeth did not get to hear the rest of Olivia's question.

Puzzled by all the excitement and just a little worried about Amy, Elizabeth fidgeted through homeroom. *There's still time for Amy to show up*, she reminded herself. *Science class isn't until just before lunch*. But it wasn't at all like Amy to be late, especially on the day they were supposed to turn in a project. Maybe she should go to the pay phone outside the principal's office and give Amy a call.

At last, homeroom was over. Elizabeth looked for Olivia, interested in hearing the rest of her question, but Olivia was talking animatedly with Ken Matthews and Sandra Ferris. Elizabeth gathered her books, started down the aisle, and bumped into Caroline Pearce. Caroline was the biggest gossip in Sweet Valley, but even though she usually knew the latest news, she had a knack for getting most of the details wrong.

"Elizabeth, you're just the person I wanted to see," Caroline said importantly. "I'm hoping that you'll be able to fill me in on some of the details."

Elizabeth glanced at her watch, thinking that if she hurried, there might still be time to call Amy before her next class. "I'm sorry, Caroline," she said, "I don't have time to talk right now. I have to make an important phone call."

Caroline tossed her straight red hair over her shoulder. "Oh, but you *have* to tell me, Elizabeth," she insisted, her green eyes sparkling with curiosity. "You're probably the only person who knows the actual truth." She waved her hand at Olivia, Ken, and Sandra, who were still huddled together. "Everybody's talking about it, but they're all just guessing."

Elizabeth frowned. "Guessing about what?"

"About what happened last night, of course," Caroline said impatiently. "Come on, Elizabeth, you can tell me. You know how important it is for people to have the facts in a terrible situation like this. Otherwise, all kinds of weird stories start going around." Caroline leaned forward conspiratorially. "And of course, that's just what's happening now. Nobody knows for sure what happened last night, so everyone's imagining the worst."

"The worst about *what*?" Elizabeth demanded. "What are you talking about?"

Caroline stared at her, open-mouthed. "You mean, you haven't heard what happened to Amy Sutton? Elizabeth, where have you *been* all morning?"

Elizabeth felt her mouth go dry. "Something's happened to Amy?" she cried anxiously. "What? What happened?"

Caroline paused dramatically before answering. "Amy's house burned down last night."

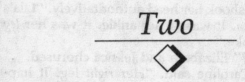

Two

"Amy's . . . house burned down?" Elizabeth gulped.

"To the ground," Caroline replied with satisfaction. "It was a terrible fire. It raged for hours and hours. Six Sweet Valley fire trucks were called to the scene, and the firemen were there all night. But they couldn't save anything. The fire was so hot that they just had to let it burn."

"But Amy!" Elizabeth cried frantically. "What happened to Amy?"

"That's the most terrible thing of all," Caroline said in a hushed voice.

At that moment, Jessica came up, her blue-green eyes wide with excitement. "Elizabeth," she cried, "have you heard—?"

"Caroline is just telling me," Elizabeth said, trying desperately to remain calm. "Caroline, what happened to Amy?"

"Elizabeth, you won't believe it," Jessica said. "Lila told me that Amy broke her ankle. She was hurrying down the stairs to get out of the house and—"

Caroline shook her head authoritatively. "Lila's wrong, Jessica. It wasn't her ankle. It was her *leg* that Amy broke."

"Her *leg*?" Elizabeth and Jessica chorused.

"Yes," Caroline said. "Her *right* leg. It happened when she jumped out her window. She was trapped in her bedroom by the *roaring* flames, and the only way out was through the window."

"The *window*?" Jessica screeched. "Amy jumped out of her *window*? Don't be silly, Caroline. Amy's room is on the second floor. It must be at least twenty feet off the ground!"

"Thirty," Caroline corrected. "That's why she broke her leg. Thirty feet is a long way to jump. The firemen had a net, but she missed it."

"I can't believe it," Jessica whispered.

Elizabeth swallowed hard. "I can't believe it either." She felt ice-cold. Amy had asked her to spend the night. If it hadn't been for the special dinner with her family, she would have accepted the invitation. *She* might have been trapped in the burning house, along with Amy!

Caroline looked curiously at Elizabeth. "I'm

really surprised that you hadn't heard all of this already, Elizabeth. After all, Amy Sutton *is* your best friend. I'd have thought that she would have called you by now and told you all about it." She paused. "That is, if she was *able* to call."

"Able to call?" Jessica asked.

"They took her to the hospital, you know," Caroline replied. "In an ambulance, with the sirens going and everything. Who knows what else might be wrong with her? Maybe she didn't call because she's—"

Elizabeth sucked in her breath. "Caroline," she interrupted, "are you *sure* you've got your story straight?"

Caroline looked huffy. "Of course I'm sure, Elizabeth. I heard every word of it from Patrick Morris. He said that Jimmy Underwood walked past Amy's house on the way to school this morning and saw that it had burned down. Tim Davis was there—he lives on the next block. He told Jimmy exactly what happened, and Jimmy told Patrick just what Tim told him. So the story has got to be true. You can ask Tim if you want to."

At that moment, the first period bell rang.

"Oh, no," Jessica gasped. "I'm going to be late to class—again!"

But even though Elizabeth always made it a point to get to class on time, this morning she couldn't worry about being late. She had something much more terrible to worry about. Her best friend's house had burned down and she was in the hospital with a broken leg—and maybe with something worse. It was the most awful news Elizabeth had ever heard.

The worst part about it was that Elizabeth couldn't be sure whether what she had heard was the truth or not. What had really happened to Amy? If the Suttons' house had burned down, where would Amy and her family live? Would Amy have to stay with her grandmother, who lived far away? Would Elizabeth ever see her friend again?

For the rest of the morning, it seemed as if nobody talked about anything but the fire. Sixth, seventh, and eighth graders gathered in groups in the hallway to compare notes. Friends continually stopped Elizabeth to ask her if she had heard from Amy. Over and over again, Elizabeth had to repeat that she knew only what she had heard from other people.

And the stories Elizabeth heard were getting wilder and wilder. After English class, Ken Matthews came over to Elizabeth.

"I'm really worried about Amy," he said. "Lois Waller told me that she didn't just break her right leg, she broke *both* legs!"

"I heard that story too," Winston Egbert added. "Is it true, Elizabeth?"

"I don't know," Elizabeth admitted miserably. She hurried off to math class, where Julie

Porter stopped her. Julie worked on the *Sixers* with Elizabeth and Amy.

"Nora Mercandy just told me that she walked by the Suttons' house on her way to school this morning," Julie reported sadly. "There was nothing left but a stack of bricks where the fireplace had been."

Elizabeth bit her lip.

"Amy was taken to the hospital in an ambulance," Julie added. "Nora heard that from Tim Davis, who lives pretty close to Amy."

By the end of math class, Elizabeth had heard so many stories that she didn't know what to believe. Each story was more scary than the one before, and Elizabeth was so worried about Amy that she could hardly think. But when it was time for science class, she had a new worry to think about. She and Amy had spent almost two weeks working on their science project. And now, with the Suttons' house burning down, their science project was probably burned as well. Unless somebody had managed to save it from the flames, she and Amy had no science project to hand in.

Before class began, Elizabeth went up to Ms. Caxton's desk. "Ms. Caxton," she said, "everybody's saying that there was a fire at Amy's house last night."

"I know, Elizabeth," Ms. Caxton said soberly. "I've heard some of the stories. Mr. Edwards is checking to see what he can find out." Mr. Edwards was the vice principal of Sweet Valley Middle School.

"Well, Amy and I were working on our project at her house. It was ready to hand in today, but if her house burned, then it probably burned, too."

Ms. Caxton put a comforting hand on Elizabeth's shoulder. "Let's wait until we know what really happened before we decide what to do, Elizabeth. The final day on this science unit is next Tuesday. If your work was damaged in the fire, you can have until then to turn it in. You can take your quiz then, too."

Elizabeth felt relieved. The project was one worry she could put aside for the moment. As Elizabeth walked to her seat, Peter DeHaven told her that he had heard that Amy would be in the hospital for at least a month. Elizabeth immediately tensed up. If that were true, it meant that Amy wouldn't be able to work on the science project at all. Elizabeth would have to reconstruct the entire project by herself.

That afternoon after school, Elizabeth caught up with Sophia Rizzo. Sophia was also a good friend of Amy's.

"Will you walk with me to Amy's house?" Elizabeth asked urgently. "I've got to see what happened. I haven't been able to think of anything but the fire all day long."

Sophia nodded, her brown eyes wide with

worry. "Do you suppose it's true, Elizabeth?"

Elizabeth shook her head. "I'm not sure about anything," she said. "I've heard so many different stories that I don't know what to think anymore."

The girls hurried as fast as they could to the Suttons' house. A half a block away, Sophia stopped. "Look," she said, pointing. "There's a bunch of people standing around on the sidewalk."

Elizabeth broke into a run. When she got to the place where Amy's house had stood, she gasped. There was nothing left but a pile of burned bricks and a heap of smoldering ashes.

"Oh, no!" Sophia breathed. "It wasn't just a rumor. Amy's house really did burn down!"

Elizabeth nodded. "But we still don't know what happened to Amy."

"You haven't heard what happened to Amy?" Tim Davis asked as he approached them, carrying a basketball.

"We've heard a lot of things," Sophia said.

"What we need is the truth," Elizabeth added.

"Well, the truth is that Amy broke both legs and both arms," Tim said. He bounced the ball on the sidewalk. "I know, because I woke up when the ambulance drove past our house."

"But you didn't actually *see* Amy?" Elizabeth asked. "I mean, you didn't see how badly she was hurt?"

Tim shook his head. "No, but I saw the ambulance when I looked out the window. I heard the part about her broken legs and arms from Jimmy Underwood and Patrick Morris."

Elizabeth sighed. She wasn't any closer to knowing the truth than she'd been that morning.

Ten minutes later, Elizabeth opened the front door of the Wakefields' house. "Hi, Mom," she called. "I'm home." Elizabeth was anxious to talk to her mother. Maybe Mrs. Wakefield had heard what had happened last night.

Elizabeth entered the kitchen where a tray of tempting, fresh-baked cookies sat on the counter, but the kitchen was empty. She opened the door to the den and stuck her head in. "Mom?" she asked. "Where are you?"

She heard her mother's voice call out. "Up here, Elizabeth. I'm in your room."

"Mom," Elizabeth called, hurrying up the stairs. "Has there been a message from Amy?"

The door to Elizabeth's room was open and Elizabeth went in. "Mom," she said, "have you heard—?" Then she stopped.

Mrs. Wakefield was sitting in a chair beside the bed. In the bed, propped up against the pillows, lay Amy. A big white cast covered her right arm from her elbow to her hand, leaving only her fingers sticking out. She looked pale and tired, but she brightened when she saw Elizabeth.

"Amy!" Elizabeth cried. "I'm so glad to see you!" She ran over to the bed. "Are you all right?"

"I'm OK," Amy said. "Except for this broken arm. My mom and dad are all right, too." Her pale blue-gray eyes filled with tears. "But everything is gone, Elizabeth. Our house, all of my clothes, my books, and my stuffed animals. My baton, too." She glanced down at her broken arm. "Not that I would be able to use it for a while," she added sadly, while one tear trickled down her cheek.

"But at least you don't have two broken arms and two broken legs," Elizabeth said quietly. "And you're not going to be in the hospital for a month."

"*What?*" Amy asked, her eyes widening in surprise.

"There were quite a few rumors going around about what happened," Elizabeth told her.

Mrs. Wakefield stood up. "I think I'll go downstairs and fix dinner," she said. "Amy, do you feel up to eating some fried chicken? You can have dinner on a tray, here in Elizabeth's room."

Amy loved Mrs. Wakefield's fried chicken. "Sure!" she said, her face brightening. "That would be great, if it's not too much trouble."

Mrs. Wakefield leaned over and smoothed Amy's limp blond hair away from her forehead. "Not at all," she said with a smile. "Anyway, it's not every day that we have a guest. If you're not too tired, Amy, why don't you tell Elizabeth the whole story?" she asked as she left the room.

Elizabeth sat down on the bed. "What happened?" she asked. "Tell me all about it. That is, if you're feeling up to it."

"There's not much to tell," Amy said with a shrug. "The fire started in the family room. The smoke alarm went off and woke everybody up. By the time I got my sneakers on, I could smell smoke. When I got downstairs, Dad was phoning the fire department." She shook her head. "The fire must have spread awfully fast after that. By the time the fire trucks got to the house, it was just too late to do anything. I'm afraid our science project is all burned up, Elizabeth. Our wonderful chart, our typed report, everything."

"Don't worry, Amy. I talked to Ms. Caxton this morning," Elizabeth told her. "She said that we could have an extension for a week from tomorrow."

"Well, that's one less thing I have to worry about," Amy said.

"How did the fire start?" Elizabeth asked.

Amy shifted uncomfortably. "Nobody knows. At least, not yet. Mom said the insurance company will investigate and do a report." She glanced at the plate of cookies that sat on Elizabeth's night-table. "Do you think I could have another cookie?"

Elizabeth handed her one and took one for herself. "It must be terrible to lose all of your things," she said. "But still, it must have been pretty exciting to see the firemen at work with their hoses and axes."

Amy sighed and took a bite of her cookie. "Maybe. But I really didn't get to see any of it. After I broke my arm, our next-door neighbor made me lie down on her sofa until the ambulance came. I thought that was silly, because my arm didn't hurt very much. It's not a bad break. It should heal fast. The doctor says that I can go to school tomorrow, as long as I don't have a temperature."

Elizabeth glanced down at Amy's cast. "How *did* you break it? Caroline Pearce said that it happened when you jumped out of your bedroom window. She said the firemen had set up a net but that you missed it."

Amy gave a disgusted laugh. "Caroline Pearce said that? You know better than to believe anything *she* says."

"There wasn't any net?"

"No, and no jump, either," Amy replied. "Anyway, if I'd jumped, I wouldn't have gotten hurt. My window isn't more than ten feet off the ground and there are bushes under it." She sighed. "There *were* bushes under it."

"Then how did you break your arm?" Elizabeth asked.

Amy looked embarrassed. "If I tell you, will you promise not to tell anybody? I don't want people to think I'm a total idiot."

Elizabeth nodded.

"I didn't tie my shoelace," Amy whispered.

"I tripped over it when I came down the front steps."

Elizabeth tried not to smile. Amy's mother was always reminding her to tie her shoelaces so that she wouldn't trip. "But you *did* get to ride in an ambulance," Elizabeth pointed out.

Amy nodded. "At least that was exciting. They put me on a stretcher. Mom rode in front, and the ambulance driver turned on the lights and the siren. I think the story is going to be on TV, too. A crew from Mom's TV station was there, taking pictures." Amy's mother was a reporter for the local television station.

"So now what?" Elizabeth asked. "What is your family going to do?"

Amy sighed. "I wish I knew," she said, sounding depressed. "Dad and Mom are staying with my uncle. They're going to start looking for a new house right away."

"What about you?" Elizabeth asked.

"That's the good part." Amy smiled. "My mom asked your mom if I could move in with you for a while. Your mom said yes."

"That's *great!*" Elizabeth exclaimed. "You can have the bed, and I'll sleep on a cot. And you can wear my clothes and I'll help you to do things. It won't be easy for you the first few days, getting used to that cast."

Amy looked at her gratefully. "Elizabeth, has anyone ever told you that you are absolutely the most terrific friend in the whole world?"

Elizabeth laughed. "Can a terrific friend ask a big favor?"

"Sure," Amy said. "Anything you want." She held up her broken arm. "Well, almost anything."

Elizabeth went to her desk and got a red marker. "I want to be the first person to sign your cast."

With a flourish, Elizabeth wrote, "Get well soon, Amy," and signed it, "Love, Elizabeth." Then she drew a big red heart around what she had written.

Three

◇

"Wow, I didn't know it was so late," Jessica said. She sipped the last of her milkshake. She and three of the Unicorns had been enjoying an after-school treat at Casey's Place, an ice cream parlor at the mall that was one of the Unicorns' favorite hang-outs. She turned to Mary Wallace. "What time is your mom picking us up, Mary?"

"In five minutes," Mary answered. "We'd better get going."

"Remember what we agreed," Ellen Riteman reminded Jessica. "The minute you find out what really happened to Amy Sutton, call us."

"That's right," Lila Fowler put in. She tossed her light brown hair over her shoulder. "We can't trust the rumors flying around. We need to find out the truth."

Jessica shook her head. "I still don't understand why you're suddenly so interested in Amy," she said. Lila had never liked Amy.

Lila shrugged. "I'm interested in anything that goes on in Sweet Valley. Unfortunately, nothing very exciting has happened in the last few weeks— except for the Suttons' fire."

Mary Wallace nodded. "And anyway, Amy *is* a member of the Boosters."

Ellen looked cross. Jessica knew that Ellen didn't like to be reminded that Amy was a member of the Boosters. For a little while, she'd been grateful to Amy for rescuing her from a kidnapper in an old run-down house where she, Lila, and Jessica thought Mary was being held captive. But after a time Ellen had forgotten all about being grateful and had gone back to being hostile.

Ellen brought the subject back to Sweet Valley. "Things *have* been dead around here lately," she said in a bored voice. "There haven't been any big parties since Aaron's. We need a party to liven things up."

"I wish *I* could give one, but I can't," Lila said regretfully. "We're remodeling the patio, and the gardens are completely torn up. I can't even use the swimming pool."

"I can't give a party either," Ellen said. "My mother will be out of town for a week." She frowned. "Don't we know *anybody* who could give a good party?"

Everybody thought for a minute but nobody could think of anyone.

Then Jessica stood up. "Come on, Mary. We've got to meet your mother. We'll talk about the party some other time, you guys."

On the way home, Mrs. Wallace detoured past the Suttons' house so that they could see what had really happened. Jessica's eyes widened when she saw the heap of blackened bricks where the fireplace had been, and the pile of ashes.

"How awful!" she exclaimed.

"It is terrible," Mrs. Wallace said. "I wonder where the Suttons will be living?"

"I feel sorry for Amy," Mary said soberly. "Do you suppose she was able to save anything? I wonder if she has anything to wear?"

Jessica shuddered, thinking of her own stuffed closet. "I can't imagine anything more horrible than losing my clothes. Except maybe losing my new Melody Power tape," she added, "or my autograph collection, or my Johnny Buck poster."

Mary nodded. "Listen, if you find out about Amy, call me, Jessica. Amy's a good friend."

"I'll call," Jessica promised, as they pulled up in front of the Wakefield house.

Jessica opened the front door. She was walking toward the kitchen when she heard the television in the den. Her fourteen-year-old brother Steven was sprawled on the floor in front of the set, watching a music video.

"Don't touch that," Steven said, as Jessica went to the television. "This is Dynamo's latest video."

"But I want to watch the news," Jessica protested, flipping to a different channel. "Maybe there's something on about the Suttons' fire."

Steven sat up. "Oh, yeah. I heard about that. A real bummer. Listen, Mom told me that Amy is—"

"*Sshh*," Jessica said. "The news report will tell us what *really* happened." She sat on the sofa as a picture of a burning house filled the screen. The announcer spoke in a clipped voice.

"The fire that started around five o'clock this morning, completely destroyed the home of our very own reporter, Dyan Sutton," the announcer said. "Three trucks rushed to the blaze, but the firemen were unable to put it out."

A school portrait of Amy briefly filled the screen.

"Hey," Jessica said, sitting up, "that's *Amy*!"

"I was trying to tell you," Steven said, "that—"

"Don't talk!" Jessica commanded, eyes glued to the television. The picture of Amy was followed by a shot of a still figure on a stretcher being lifted into an ambulance.

"The Suttons' twelve-year-old daughter, Amy,

was injured in the fire," the announcer continued. "She was taken to Sweet Valley Hospital. The Suttons are staying with family until they can locate a new home."

Jessica got up and flipped the channel back to Steven's music video. "Just imagine," she mused, "I know somebody who's been on TV!"

"Jess," Steven said, "I think you ought to know that—"

"Later, Steven, later," Jessica said impatiently. "I've got to call Lila and Ellen right away and tell them about the newscast." First, though, she'd run upstairs and ask Elizabeth if she had learned any other details about the fire.

Jessica pushed open Elizabeth's door and stood in the doorway, amazed.

"Amy!" she exclaimed excitedly. "I just saw you on TV! What are you doing here?"

"Didn't Steven tell you?" Elizabeth asked. "Amy's going to be staying with us for a while." She stood up. "Now that you're here to keep her company, I'll go help Mom with dinner."

"I was on TV, huh?" Amy asked, as Elizabeth left the room. "My mom's station, I bet."

Jessica nodded and sat down where Elizabeth had been. "Yes. They showed a picture of you, and then a shot of you being lifted into the ambulance." Jessica's voice was filled with awe. "You're famous, Amy."

Amy sighed. "I'd rather be famous for something other than my house burning down."

Jessica ignored Amy's remark. "Tell me all about it, Amy." she said eagerly. "I want to hear, *everything*, like what you felt when you woke up in the middle of the night and heard the crackle of flames. I'll bet it was scary."

Amy looked questioningly at Jessica. Although she and Elizabeth were best friends, it was very unusual for Elizabeth's twin to be interested in anything Amy had to say. Usually, Jessica paid as little attention to her as possible.

"Well," Amy replied after a minute, "there was a lot of smoke."

"You could have suffocated," Jessica marveled. "You're lucky to be alive."

Amy nodded, feeling strangely flattered by Jessica's interest and concern. "It was a narrow escape," she replied, even though she was probably stretching the truth a bit. There had been plenty of time to get out.

"And you broke your arm when you jumped out your window?" Jessica asked. "Caroline says that it was thirty feet to the ground."

Amy looked down at her cast. She didn't really want to tell Jessica how she had broken her arm, but she couldn't see how she could avoid it. "Actually, I—"

"You must have been scared stiff," Jessica interrupted. She shivered. "*I* would have been. I could never have jumped out of that window, even with a net."

"Well," Amy began again, "to be honest, I didn't have to—"

"That's OK, Amy," Jessica cut in with an understanding smile. "You probably shouldn't tire yourself out with too much talking. But some of the kids are really interested in hearing what happened. Do you think you'd feel up to telling them after dinner?"

"I guess," Amy said doubtfully. "But I don't have much to tell. I really don't think anybody will be interested in listening."

"Don't be silly!" Jessica exclaimed. "Everybody knows what a horrible experience the fire must have been. Just getting out alive makes you a hero!"

Elizabeth opened the door with her foot. She was carrying a big tray, loaded with food. "Mom says that the three of us can have a picnic up here, Jess. Fried chicken, potato salad, apple pie—"

"Terrific!" Jessica exclaimed, jumping up. "Listen, I'll be back in a minute. I have to call a friend or two and tell them to come over right after dinner."

Elizabeth frowned. "Come over? But maybe Amy doesn't want company tonight, Jess. She's been through a lot in the last twenty-four hours."

"It's OK, Elizabeth," Amy answered. "Maybe

the company will keep me from feeling sorry for myself."

"Whatever you say." Elizabeth carefully placed the tray on the bed. "Let me help you with your dinner," she said, unfolding Amy's napkin.

Jessica dashed off to phone Lila, Ellen, and Mary to tell them that Amy Sutton, whose picture had just appeared on television, was having dinner with her that very evening. What's more, Amy would be staying at her house indefinitely. If they wanted the real story about the fire, they could come over and hear it from Amy herself.

Elizabeth was on her way downstairs with the dinner tray, loaded with dirty dishes, when the doorbell rang. She put the tray on the kitchen counter and hurried back to answer the door. It was Mary Wallace and she was carrying her favorite stuffed teddy bear, Max.

"Hi, Mary!" Elizabeth was glad that Mary was the friend Jessica had thought of phoning.

"Jessica told me that Amy's staying with you," Mary said. "I know it's kind of childish, but I thought that she might enjoy having Max to keep her company. Is it OK if I go upstairs?"

"Sure," Elizabeth replied. "Amy will be really glad to see you. I'll be up in a few minutes."

Elizabeth was helping her mother with the dishes when the doorbell rang again. To Elizabeth's amazement, it was Lila Fowler and Ellen

Riteman. Lila was holding a box of expensive-looking chocolates.

"Good evening, Elizabeth," Lila said haughtily. "I understand that Amy Sutton is staying here."

Elizabeth was so surprised that she forgot to invite them inside. Why would two *Unicorns* want to see Amy? Amy and the Unicorns had never gotten along.

Jessica came running down the stairs. "Was that the doorbell?" she asked breathlessly.

"It's Lila and Ellen," Elizabeth said, turning around.

"Aren't you going to invite them in?" Jessica demanded. "Come on, you guys. Amy's upstairs."

Elizabeth stepped back and held the door open. With barely a glance at her, the two Unicorns followed Jessica upstairs.

"More company for Amy?" Mrs. Wakefield asked, as Elizabeth came back into the kitchen.

Elizabeth nodded. "Lila and Ellen. I hope they don't tire her out."

"Mrs. Sutton told me that the doctor wants Amy to talk about the fire as much as possible," Mrs. Wakefield replied. "Talking is good therapy."

Elizabeth nodded. She could understand why it would help Amy to talk about the fire. But she couldn't understand why the Unicorns were so anxious to listen.

*   *   *

Amy had been pleased to see Mary Wallace. She and Jessica and Mary were just starting to talk when the doorbell rang again and Jessica went to answer it. When she came back upstairs, Amy was surprised to see who was with her.

"Hello, Amy," Lila Fowler said with a warm smile. "How are you feeling? We've brought you some chocolates." Lila sat down on the foot of the bed.

"Hello, Amy," Ellen Riteman said coolly. Amy suspected that Lila had dragged Ellen to see her. She and Ellen had had a truce after Amy had rescued Ellen from the kidnapper, but it hadn't lasted very long.

"Hi," Amy answered, looking at the box of chocolates. Why were Unicorns bringing candy to *her*? But then she remembered her manners. "Thanks for the candy." She turned to Mary. "And thanks for bringing Max, Mary."

Mary blushed. "I hope you don't think a stuffed bear is too immature. He's been my friend for a long time, and I thought he might be good company for you."

Lila frowned as if she thought Mary's bear *was* terribly immature. Then she looked solicitously at Amy. "You've had a horrible experience, Amy. All of the Unicorns want you to know how sorry we are about the fire."

"That's right," Mary said. "If it will help you to talk about what happened, we'd be glad to listen."

"Tell them everything, Amy," Jessica commanded excitedly.

Amy cleared her throat. "There's not very much to tell, really."

"Yes, there is!" Jessica exclaimed. "Amy's just being modest. Before dinner, she told me how scared she was to jump out of her window. But the smoke was so heavy that she was afraid she would choke. It took a lot of courage to jump, if you ask me. Amy's a real hero."

Amy frowned. This thing about jumping out the window was beginning to be embarrassing. It was time to set the record straight, even if she had to confess that she'd really only tripped over her shoelace. "But Jessica," she began, "I didn't—"

"You must have been simply *petrified*," Lila said sympathetically. "Waking up in the middle of the night with smoke and flames all around you. I know I would have been." She poked Ellen with her elbow. "Wouldn't you have been petrified, Ellen?"

"Yes," Ellen admitted reluctantly. "I would have been scared to death."

"Actually, there wasn't a lot of flame." Amy looked cautiously at Lila. For the first time, Lila Fowler and Ellen Ritemen were actually listening to what she had to say without making a sarcastic remark. It was a new experience, and, Amy had to admit, very flattering.

"At least, there wasn't a lot of flame just *then*,"

Amy added. "There was plenty of smoke, though. Thick, choking smoke." She coughed. "I was lucky to get out alive."

Jessica looked impressed. "There must have been flames later," she said, "when the fire really got going. But by that time, of course, you were already in the ambulance." She glanced importantly at Lila and Ellen. "I saw it on TV. There was a shot of Amy on a stretcher, surrounded by ambulance attendants."

"Tell us about the ambulance ride, Amy," Mary said in a hushed voice. "Was it scary?"

Amy coughed once more. "It was, a little. The driver turned on the lights *and* the siren. There was a police escort, too."

"Really?" Lila asked respectfully.

"The driver ran all the red lights on the way to the hospital." Amy wasn't sure that that was true. From her position on the stretcher she hadn't been able to see much. But if the driver had put on the siren, he must have run the red lights too. And if he'd run the red lights, he'd probably also had a police escort.

"Wow," Mary breathed. "It sounds like a wild ride."

"I wish *I* could ride in an ambulance with the siren going, running all the red lights," Jessica said enviously. She glanced at Amy's cast. "Of course, I wouldn't want to break my arm. Even if it did mean getting my picture on TV."

"It hurt a lot," Amy said, shifting her broken arm on the covers. She winced and the Unicorns' faces were full of sympathy. She winced again.

"It must be a very bad break, to hurt that much," Mary said softly. "If I can help, please let me know."

Lila took out a purple pen. "Can I sign your cast?"

"Help yourself," Amy replied. She watched as Lila leaned over and wrote on her cast, "To Amy, Best Wishes from Lila Fowler." Under it, Lila drew a little purple unicorn, then handed the marker to Ellen. Mary signed it too, and then Jessica. Each one drew a purple unicorn under her signature.

"Do they know what caused the fire, Amy?" Lila asked conversationally.

Amy swallowed. That was a question she did not want to think about. "No," she said. "At least, not yet." She was glad when the door opened and Elizabeth came in.

Lila gave Elizabeth a cool look and stood up. "Ellen and I have to go," she announced. "When will you be back at school, Amy?"

"Tomorrow, if I don't have a temperature," Amy looked at Elizabeth. "I have to borrow some clothes, though. Everything I owned was burned up in the fire."

"You poor thing," Lila said softly. "You'll have to buy all new clothes. I'll be glad to help you shop. In the meantime, I have a few things I haven't worn lately. I'll be happy to lend them to you."

Elizabeth could not believe what she had heard. Lila Fowler was offering to loan Amy Sutton some of her designer clothes! Lila hardly even shared her clothes with Jessica, her best friend. And Amy was nodding as if she were accepting the offer! Elizabeth could see that Amy was enjoying being the center of attention. Her mother had been right. Talking about the fire—even to the Unicorns—was the best possible therapy.

Jessica went downstairs to see her friends to the door. Elizabeth glanced down at the box of chocolates on the bed. "Were you as surprised as I was when Lila and Ellen walked in with that candy?"

Amy laughed as Elizabeth helped her open the box. "I *was* pretty surprised," she admitted. "But I have to admit that it was nice of them." Amy stuck out her arm. "They signed my cast, too."

Elizabeth nodded and took one of the chocolates that Amy offered. "The Unicorns can be nice—when they want to." She almost added that they were usually nice only when they were up to something, but she caught herself. She didn't want to spoil Amy's enjoyment of the Unicorns' visit. And she couldn't imagine what scheme they could have concocted around Amy's misfortune.

Jessica came back into the room. "Well, they're gone," she said. "Now what are we going to do for the rest of the evening?"

"Eat Unicorn candy?" Amy asked with a laugh.

"How about a game of Scrabble, Amy?" Elizabeth suggested. She and Amy were both good with words and they always enjoyed challenging one another at Scrabble.

Jessica wrinkled her nose. "You know I don't like to play that game, Elizabeth. I can't think of unusual words like you can and I'm not the best speller in the world." She smiled at Amy. "But I'll play if Amy will be on my side. That will even things out."

Amy looked at Elizabeth and shrugged. "It's OK with me if it's OK with Elizabeth."

"Sure," Elizabeth said with a shrug.

"Great!" Jessica said. "I'll get my latest Johnny Buck tape. Wait till you hear it, Amy. It's outrageous!"

Elizabeth and Amy exchanged amused glances, but Elizabeth made no comment. She was glad that Jessica was being nice to Amy. It would help keep Amy's mind off the fire.

For the rest of the evening, the girls played Scrabble, nibbled on Amy's chocolates, listened to Jessica's tape, and talked. After a while, Mrs. Wakefield brought up some soft drinks and checked Amy's temperature.

"I *can* go to school tomorrow, can't I?" Amy asked anxiously.

Mrs. Wakefield looked closely at the thermometer. "I don't see why not," she said. "You girls can stay up an extra hour tonight," she added as she left the room. "But be sure that your homework is done."

Elizabeth gave a little start. "Gosh, Amy," she said, "we should get started on our science project. It's due next Tuesday." She looked at Jessica. "You don't have to hang around while we work, Jess. Our project would probably bore you."

"Are you trying to push me out?" Jessica asked with a little frown.

"Push you out?" Elizabeth asked, surprised.

"If you guys work on that project, I won't have anything to do."

"To tell you the truth, I hate the thought of constructing that project all over again," Amy said in a fretful voice.

"Well, you don't have to think about it tonight," Jessica comforted her. "You've got a whole week. Let's play another game. I'll go get my Darcy Campman tape."

Amy brightened. "Darcy Campman? Elizabeth, we can postpone the project for one night, can't we?"

So the girls played another game and listened to more music. Then Jessica went to her room, while Amy talked to her parents on the hall telephone. When it was time to go to bed, Elizabeth loaned Amy a pair of loose-fitting pajamas so that her arm would be comfortable.

Amy looked down at the pajama shirt. "I don't think I can handle buttons with my left hand," she said unhappily.

"I'll do it for you," Elizabeth offered. "I wish your house hadn't burned down, Amy. But I'm glad that you're staying with me."

Amy nodded. "I feel terrible, losing all of my clothes and stuff. But at least my family is safe. And it is good to be with my best friend."

Elizabeth smiled. "I can't make up for what you've lost, Amy. But I'll try my best to make things easier for you."

"That makes me feel better," Amy said, as she climbed back into Elizabeth's bed.

But after Elizabeth had turned out the light, and as she tried to make herself comfortable on the narrow cot, she could hear Amy crying softly in the dark.

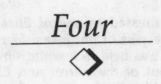

Four

Jessica tossed and turned for a long time after her light was out. She could hear Elizabeth's and Amy's voices through the bathroom that linked their bedrooms.

Jessica frowned into the darkness. Somehow, it didn't seem fair. For two whole weeks, Elizabeth had spent all of her time with Amy. Now that the Suttons' house had burned down, and Amy had moved in, Elizabeth was acting as if she didn't want to share Amy with anybody.

That night, for example, if Jessica hadn't come downstairs when she had, Elizabeth might very well have sent Lila and Ellen away. Then Elizabeth had suggested that they play Scrabble—a game she knew Jessica didn't enjoy. After that, Elizabeth had all but ordered Jessica to leave the room so that she and Amy could work on their science project.

Jessica frowned again. All she was asking was not to be left out in the cold.

Tuesday morning Jessica woke to the sound of Elizabeth and Amy giggling and talking. She got dressed in record time and went into Elizabeth's room.

Amy was dressed in one of Elizabeth's white blouses and a pair of her jeans. Her broken arm with its cast was held in a white sling. Amy was sitting in front of the mirror and Elizabeth was brushing her blond hair.

"Hi, you guys," Jessica said.

"Good morning, Jess," Elizabeth said. "I'm braiding Amy's hair. She can't do it with her arm in a cast."

"One braid is cuter than two," Jessica said helpfully. "Here, let me do it." Jessica took the hairbrush away from her sister. "Why don't you go downstairs and help Mom with breakfast, Elizabeth?"

"Good idea. Is cereal OK, Amy?"

"Sure," Amy replied. "Cereal's fine. If I were home right now, the only thing I'd get would be burned toast." She laughed half-heartedly. "That wasn't a very funny joke, I guess."

"I think Amy ought to have something a little more substantial than cereal," Jessica said importantly. "She needs to keep her strength up. Why don't you ask Mom if we can have some croissants and jam. Would you like that, Amy?"

"Croissants and jam would be fantastic," Amy agreed.

"Croissants and jam it is, then." Elizabeth went downstairs, leaving Jessica and Amy alone.

Jessica began to brush Amy's hair. "Lots of Unicorns are wearing their hair braided down the back. Yours would look nice that way. I could braid a ribbon into it, if you'd like."

"That would be nice," Amy said, sounding pleased. "But you don't have to do it if it's a lot of trouble."

"It's no trouble at all," Jessica assured her.

Amy and Jessica came into the kitchen just as Elizabeth was taking the warm croissants out of the microwave.

Amy twirled around in front of Elizabeth. "What do you think?"

"It's cute, Amy." Elizabeth raised her eyebrows. "But a *purple* ribbon?"

"It looks OK, doesn't it?" Amy asked worriedly, lifting her good hand to the back of her head. She wasn't sure she liked the purple ribbon, either. But Jessica had braided it in before she noticed its color, and she had hated to ask her to take it out.

"Your hair looks very nice, Amy," Mrs. Wakefield said with a smile.

Jessica pulled out Amy's chair. "You can get started on your breakfast. I've got a phone call to make." As Amy sat down at the table, Jessica disappeared into the hallway.

While Jessica was gone, Mrs. Wakefield poured Amy's orange juice. "Why don't I give you girls a ride to school?"

"Great, Mom," Elizabeth said. "It's probably good for Amy to take it easy for a few days."

"Thanks, Mrs. Wakefield," Amy said, as Elizabeth spread jam on her croissant.

Jessica popped back into the kitchen. "I got us a ride to school," she announced, sitting down to her breakfast.

"Mom's already offered, Jessica," Elizabeth pointed out.

"But I thought that Amy would rather ride to school in Mr. Fowler's new car," Jessica said brightly. "So I called Lila and set it up." She looked at Amy. "Wouldn't you rather ride to school in the Fowlers' new car, Amy?"

"Actually, I'd rather ride with Elizabeth," Amy replied.

"Oh, don't worry. It's a big car," Jessica assured her. "There'll be plenty of room for Elizabeth, too."

Mrs. Wakefield laughed and reached for her briefcase. "I'm sure that all three of you would rather ride in style. See you this evening."

When Mr. Fowler pulled up in front of the Wakefield's house a few minutes later, Amy saw that the new car, big as it was, was already crammed full of Unicorns. Lila and Ellen were in the front seat, and Tamara Chase and Mary Wallace were in the back.

"I don't think there's room for three more," Elizabeth noted with a laugh. "I'll walk."

"I'm sorry, Elizabeth," Jessica whispered. "I didn't know that Lila was going to stop for anybody else."

Amy pulled back. "I don't want to ride if Elizabeth can't. I'll walk too."

"That's OK, Amy," Elizabeth said, "it's a good idea for you to ride to school this morning. We can walk together tomorrow or the next day."

"Elizabeth's right, Amy," Lila said sounding almost concerned. "You can sit up here with me so that your arm won't get mashed. Ellen, you get in the back."

With a small frown, Ellen got out of the car and climbed into the back seat with Jessica and the others. Amy slid in beside Lila.

"I hope you're feeling better this morning, Amy," Lila said, as she helped Amy buckle her seat belt.

"Yes, thanks." Amy could not believe that she was actually riding to school in Mr. Fowler's new car. She felt grateful to Jessica for having arranged it, and to Elizabeth for having insisted that she accept the ride. Amy turned awkwardly to wave goodbye to Elizabeth, but she was already out of sight.

* * *

Elizabeth got to homeroom and looked around for Amy. After a minute she spotted her, completely surrounded by a group of kids. Julie Porter was standing on the outskirts of the group.

"Hi, Elizabeth." Julie joined her friend. "I'm glad Amy could come to school this morning."

Sophia Rizzo joined them. "Me too. I was happy to find out that she didn't have two broken legs!"

"A broken arm is bad enough," Elizabeth observed. Though Amy was across the room, Elizabeth could hear her explaining that a cloud of thick, choking smoke had completely filled the burning house just before she escaped.

Caroline Pearce put her hand to her throat and pretended to gag. "It makes me choke just to *hear* about it!"

"It *was* pretty awful," Amy replied. "I thought I'd never stop coughing."

That's odd, Elizabeth thought. She didn't remember that part of Amy's story. In fact, she thought Amy had said that she had only *smelled* smoke. Just then the bell rang and the group around Amy broke up reluctantly.

"What an exciting story," Julie said, as they made their way to their desks.

"I was hoping Amy would tell the part about jumping out of the window." Sophia turned to Elizabeth. "Wasn't that how she broke her arm, Elizabeth?"

Elizabeth felt a little uncomfortable. She knew that Amy was embarrassed by the fact that she had tripped over her shoelace. And she didn't want to be the one to tell her friend's embarrassing secret.

"You'll have to ask Amy," she answered. "I'm sure she'll be glad to tell you the whole story."

Meanwhile, Amy was enjoying the attention she was getting from the kids at school. It felt good to have so many people—even people she hardly knew—listening to her so attentively.

And Amy realized that the attention also helped to keep her mind off more troubling matters. When everyone was gathered around her, being supportive and sympathetic, she didn't have to think about how much it hurt to have lost everything. And she didn't have to think about the way in which the fire had started. If only she'd remembered to take out the fireplace ashes, instead of just shoveling them into that paper bag! Because of her carelessness, her family was homeless. And when the insurance company made its report, everyone would know what she had done. Amy's secret was too horrible to tell anybody, even Elizabeth.

So when the kids gathered around to hear what had happened and to ask about her arm, Amy just kept talking as long as they would listen. She figured that when her parents found out that she was responsible for the fire, she'd need all of the friends she could get.

Amy was glad to see Elizabeth when they met in the cafeteria for lunch.

"I'll carry your tray, Amy," Elizabeth offered as they got into line.

"Thank you," Amy said gratefully. She was just asking Elizabeth to pick up a plate of lasagna when a group of Unicorns, led by Janet Howell, the president of the club, came up to them.

"Amy," Jessica announced, "Janet would like you to eat lunch with us at the Unicorner." The Unicorner was the group's favorite lunch table. "Some of the Unicorns haven't heard your story yet, and they're just dying to hear every detail," Jessica added.

"You can come if you want to, Elizabeth," Janet said graciously.

Amy felt cornered. She hadn't yet straightened out the story about how she had broken her arm. Only Elizabeth knew that she'd tripped over her shoelace. Everybody else thought it had happened when she jumped out her window.

Amy was distracted by Julie who came hurrying up to the group. "Elizabeth," she said, "Mr. Bowman wants to see you right after lunch. He has an idea for the *Sixers* he wants to discuss with you."

"Thanks, Julie," Elizabeth said. "I wonder what it is?"

"You could go now, Elizabeth," Amy suggested quickly. "I'm sure I can manage."

"I'll help!" Jessica took Amy's tray from Elizabeth.

"OK. I think I will go and see him now. I can eat lunch when I get back." Elizabeth hurried off.

"What would you like to eat, Amy?" Jessica asked.

"Lasagna, please."

"How about some chocolate cake?" Lila asked helpfully.

Amy nodded. She couldn't believe it. Jessica Wakefield and the Unicorns were falling all over themselves to get her lunch!

Amy walked with Janet across the cafeteria. Jessica followed, carrying Amy's tray. At the Unicorn table, Lila pulled out a chair for Amy, right next to Janet, while Mary got her a napkin. Tamara Chase made a special trip for some ice cream, and Jessica opened Amy's milk. Amy wanted to pinch herself. She'd never had so much attention in her whole life—from *Unicorns*, too!

After all of the Unicorns were seated, Janet invited Amy to tell her story. "Tell it from the beginning," she instructed. "And don't leave out a *single* detail."

Jessica leaned forward. "Especially tell about jumping out of the window," she urged. "That's the part that everybody wants to hear." She turned to Kimberly Haver, who was sitting next to her. "That's how Amy broke her arm," she explained.

"That's right," Mary said sympathetically. "The

doctor said that it was a terrible break. It might take months and months to heal."

Tamara looked at Amy. "Do they know what caused the fire?"

Amy felt her stomach tighten. She hated that question. But before she had a chance to make up an answer, Ellen came hurrying up with her lunch tray.

"Hi, everybody," she said, smiling around the table at everyone but Amy. "I've just been talking to Brooke Dennis about the party she and her father are throwing."

Lila put down her fork. "What party?" she demanded. "Brooke Dennis is having a party?"

"All *right!*" Tamara Chase cried excitedly.

Brooke Dennis had moved to Sweet Valley several months earlier. Her father was a famous Hollywood screenwriter, and he had hired the firm at which Mrs. Wakefield worked to redecorate the house they had moved into. For a while, Amy remembered, Brooke had acted terribly stuck-up and the other kids had been so angry they had played a nasty trick on her. But then Elizabeth had discovered that Brooke was really very lonely and she'd made friends with her. Afterwards, Brooke had become someone that everybody really liked.

"Well, she's *thinking* about a party, anyway," Ellen corrected herself. "She and her father have just finished redecorating that big house they moved into and they want to show it off."

"That's right," Jessica put in importantly. "Mr. Dennis is my mother's client. She's been in charge of the decorating."

Ellen looked pointedly at Lila. "Speaking of decorating, I think I could convince Brooke that she ought to let the Unicorns help with the party. That is, if we aren't too busy with other things." Ellen shifted her glance to Amy.

Lila laughed. "Don't be silly, Ellen. I'm never too busy to think about a party." Lila turned toward Amy. "But for now, I want to hear Amy's story again. It's *very* exciting."

So Amy told her story to the group of spell-bound Unicorns, while Ellen ate her lunch, scowling and pretending not to listen.

That afternoon after school, Amy waited at her locker for Elizabeth, so that they could go to the regular *Sixers* meeting together.

"Hi, Amy," Elizabeth called as she approached. "Want me to open your locker for you?"

"Please! That's one of the things I can't manage very easily with this cast."

As Elizabeth turned the dial on the combination lock she said, "Listen, I've got a great idea. How about you and I getting together and writing a front-page story on the fire for the *Sixers*? We could do the story as an interview."

Amy frowned. "An interview?"

"Sure," Elizabeth said eagerly. "I'll ask you questions, such as what caused the fire and how you and your parents got out of the house. And you answer them."

Amy shook her head. Elizabeth would have to ask certain questions about the fire that Amy did not want to answer. "I . . . don't think I want to do an interview, Elizabeth," she said. "I'd like to do the story, but I'd rather write it by myself."

"But don't you think an interview format would be more exciting? And it would be less work for you because we'd be writing it together. In fact, we could do it tonight, after dinner. We could have a lot of fun."

Amy straightened her shoulders. "We're already doing our science project together, Elizabeth," she said sharply. "Do we have to do *everything* together?"

Elizabeth looked hurt and Amy immediately felt guilty. But she didn't know how else to avoid having to tell Elizabeth her terrible secret.

"No, not if you don't want to," Elizabeth said quietly.

"Well, I don't," Amy replied. "I'd rather write it in my own way, if you don't mind."

"OK, if that's the way you want it."

The two girls walked together in silence to the *Sixers* meeting. When they arrived, Elizabeth suggested to Mr. Bowman that they run a front-page story about the fire that had destroyed Amy's house.

"Hey, that's a terrific idea, Elizabeth," Mr. Bowman exclaimed. "Amy, why don't you and Elizabeth work on the story together? An interview format would be very interesting."

"I . . . I'd rather write the story myself," Amy said, looking directly at Mr. Bowman. "I think it would be better that way." She wished that she could think of a convincing reason *why* it would be better, but she couldn't.

Mr. Bowman shrugged. "If you want to write it yourself, that's all right with me," he said. "Why don't you turn it in by Friday. We won't really need the article until next week, but I'd like to have a look at it over the weekend."

The rest of the meeting seemed to go on forever, and Amy was glad when it was over. But as she and Elizabeth walked home together, there didn't seem to be anything to say. She wanted to apologize to Elizabeth, but she couldn't without telling her the real reasons why she didn't want to do the interview. She didn't want the embarrassing truth about how she'd really broken her arm to appear in the *Sixers*. She didn't want to have to back down from the story she'd told the Unicorns and the other kids at school. And worst of all, she didn't want to have to answer the question, "How did the fire start?"

That was one question and answer she could not bear to think about.

Five

Elizabeth was still feeling very hurt when she and Amy got home that afternoon. It wasn't really their difference of opinion over the newspaper story that bothered her. She still thought that the interview was a better idea, but it *was* Amy's story and she should write it in whichever way she wanted. What really bothered Elizabeth was the way in which Amy had made it clear that she just didn't want Elizabeth to be involved.

Mrs. Wakefield was taking a mixing bowl out of a cabinet when the girls came into the kitchen. "Hello, girls," she said cheerfully. "Amy, if you'll tell me your favorite cake, Elizabeth and I will bake it for dessert tonight. Do you have some time to help me, Elizabeth?"

"I guess so," Elizabeth replied unenthusiastically. She wasn't really sure that she felt like doing something special for Amy just now.

"Chocolate, please," Amy said. "I wish I could help you, but I'm afraid that with this cast I'm not much good at anything."

"Hi, everybody!' Jessica burst into the kitchen, her arms full of clothes. "Hey, Amy, guess what I've got! Tons and tons of really neat outfits!"

"For me?" Amy asked brightly.

Jessica nodded. "From the Unicorns. Come on! Let's go upstairs and try them on!"

When Amy and Jessica had gone, Mrs. Wakefield turned to Elizabeth. "I thought you'd be pleased to make a cake for Amy."

Elizabeth sat down at the kitchen table. "I am, I guess. But I'm confused. Amy acted kind of strange today."

"Strange?"

"Well, I suggested to Amy that we do an interview about the fire for the *Sixers*," Elizabeth replied. "But Amy wants to write the story herself." Elizabeth didn't want to tell her mother what Amy had said about their not having to do everything together. She didn't want to get Amy in any sort of trouble, and some part of her thought that maybe she had overreacted to Amy's comment.

Mrs. Wakefield put her hand on Elizabeth's shoulder. "When people suffer a loss as large as Amy's," she said quietly, "they sometimes act in ways they otherwise wouldn't. What Amy needs right now is a patient and understanding friend."

Elizabeth frowned. "I'll try."

Mrs. Wakefield hugged her. "I'm sure you'll do your best," she said confidently. "Now, how about that cake?"

But being understanding turned out to be harder than Elizabeth expected. When she went upstairs after the cake had been put in the oven, Elizabeth discovered that her usually neat room had become a total mess. Jessica and Amy had been trying on the Unicorns' outfits as well as Elizabeth's and Jessica's clothing. Tops, skirts, and pants were strewn over everything.

"I hope you don't mind Amy trying on your stuff," Jessica said, coming from her room with another armful of outfits. Amy was in the bathroom, turning in front of the full-length mirror. She was wearing Elizabeth's best blue dress.

"Not really," Elizabeth said. "What I *do* mind is the mess." Messes weren't news to Amy, or to Jessica. Neither one of them ever cleaned their rooms until their mothers gave them strict orders to do so.

"Don't worry, we'll clean it up," Jessica said carelessly as she joined Amy in the bathroom. "Amy, why don't you try on my red top with Lila's white pants?"

After a delicious dinner, topped off by chocolate cake, Jessica and Amy rushed back upstairs to try on more clothes. Elizabeth followed slowly, puzzled by their friendly chatter. Jessica and Amy had never gotten along very well before and now they were acting as if they were the best of friends. But as long as Amy had to stay with them, Elizabeth figured it was better for Amy and Jessica to be friends than to be enemies.

Elizabeth pushed a big pile of clothes off her desk and chair and took out her notes for the science project. "Amy," she called, "maybe it'd be a good idea for us to get going on our science project tonight. It's due next Tuesday."

There was a sudden silence in the bathroom. Then Jessica stuck her head out the door. "Does Amy have to do it right this minute, Elizabeth?" she asked. "We're conducting an experiment."

"I guess not. I've got some math problems to do." Elizabeth opened her book and tried to shut out the sound of excited giggling. She'd been working for nearly a half hour when Jessica stepped through the bathroom door with a flourish.

"Well, what do you think?" she asked triumphantly, standing aside so that Elizabeth could see Amy. "Doesn't Amy look *cute*?"

Elizabeth blinked. The girl standing beside Jessica didn't look *anything* like Amy. She was wearing a purple designer top that must have come from Lila, Jessica's pink drawstring-waist pants, and a string of pink beads that Elizabeth recognized as Mary's. Her blond hair was tied back with a purple ribbon, and she was wearing lip gloss and a little bit of blusher.

"Well?" Amy asked.

"Say you like my newest creation, Elizabeth," Jessica commanded.

Elizabeth wasn't at all sure that she liked Amy in makeup and all dressed up in the Unicorns' clothes. But she didn't want to hurt Amy's feelings. "You look fine, Amy. But doesn't all that purple make you feel like a Unicorn?"

"And what's wrong with feeling like a Unicorn?" Jessica asked defensively, lifting her chin. "Or with looking like one?"

Elizabeth waited for Amy to tell Jessica exactly what she thought about the Unicorns, but she said nothing. Instead, Amy giggled.

"I know what we need!" Jessica flopped down on the pile of clothes that covered Elizabeth's bed. "We need a snack! Trying on clothes always makes me hungry."

"We only finished dinner a little while ago," Elizabeth objected. "Anyway, Amy and I have some homework to do." She looked pointedly around the room. "And you promised to clean up this mess."

Amy flopped down beside Jess. "Well, I *would* like another piece of chocolate cake."

"That's a terrific idea, Amy. Elizabeth, if you'll get the cake, Amy and I will start cleaning up your room."

Elizabeth closed her book. "It's a deal," she said promptly. When the room was cleaned up and they had finished their cake, maybe Amy would be ready to start on the science project.

But when Elizabeth got back upstairs with the three pieces of chocolate cake on a tray, she discovered that Amy and Jessica had only gotten as far as shoving the clothes off the bed and onto the floor. Now they were sitting crosslegged on the bed, setting up the Monopoly board.

"Thanks, Elizabeth," Amy said, accepting the cake Elizabeth handed her. "This sure would taste good with a glass of milk."

"All right, but what about the room?" Elizabeth asked. "I thought you guys were going to clean it up."

"Amy's arm was hurting," Jessica explained, counting out Monopoly money. "Besides, we wanted to play a game. Bring me a glass of milk too, Elizabeth."

Elizabeth noticed that the game board was only set up for two players. "You don't want me to play?"

Jessica looked surprised. "I thought you had to do some homework."

"You're right. I do," Elizabeth sighed. She could at least look over her notes for the science project and try to figure out what she and Amy had to do.

But when she settled down to her work, Elizabeth found it very hard to concentrate with Jessica and Amy squealing and laughing over the game. Finally, Elizabeth picked up a magazine and sat on her cot to read.

Suddenly, Jessica looked up from the game. "That's the magazine that's got a picture of that cute outfit," Jessica said, nodding toward Elizabeth. "Remember, Amy? I was telling you about it."

"Really? I'd love to see it," Amy said.

"Can I have the magazine for a minute, Elizabeth?" Jessica stuck out her hand and Elizabeth passed her the magazine.

Jessica and Amy forgot totally about their game as they leafed through Elizabeth's magazine and chattered about clothes. Eventually, the conversation turned to boys. Jessica went on and on about Aaron Dallas, while Amy gushed about Ken Matthews. They seemed to be having an enormous amount of fun.

But Elizabeth wasn't having any fun at all. Amy was behaving exactly like a Unicorn. And Elizabeth could not help but feel resentful. How long was she going to have to put up with this strange new situation? Her room was a horrible mess, her privacy had been invaded, and her best friend's personality was rapidly changing—for the worse. For a moment, Elizabeth wasn't even sure that she had a best friend any longer.

But then Elizabeth remembered what her mother had said. A terrible loss like the one Amy had suffered could have a big effect on a person's behavior. Elizabeth took a deep breath and vowed that she would make an extra effort to stop feeling hurt and resentful.

So when they were finally ready to go to bed, Elizabeth took the purple ribbon out of Amy's hair, helped her to button her pajamas, and put away the Monopoly set that Jessica had carelessly left behind.

As Amy got into bed, Elizabeth said, "I've been thinking, Amy. I know that you don't want to do an interview for the *Sixers*. But if you'd like, I'll be glad to help you write your story."

"I don't *need* any help writing the story," Amy said quickly, her face turned from Elizabeth. "But I would like a glass of water."

After Elizabeth gave Amy a glass of water, she did something she hadn't done for a very long time. She took her old stuffed koala bear from the shelf, the one she used to sleep with when she was a child, and set it down on the pillow of the uncomfortable cot. Perhaps it was childish, but snuggling her friendly old bear made her feel a little less lonely and a little less hurt.

Later that night, Elizabeth woke to the sound of Amy crying. She got up and turned on the light. "Amy," she asked softly, "can I get you another glass of water?"

Amy shook her head. "No. I had a bad dream, that's all."

Elizabeth turned off the light and crawled back onto the cot. Within a few minutes she was asleep, her koala bear in her arms.

For the next two days, Elizabeth continued to appear patient and understanding. But on the inside, she was anything but relaxed. For one thing, Elizabeth was really worried about the science project. Even though she kept reminding Amy that it was due the following Tuesday, Amy made absolutely no effort to work on it. Instead, she and Jessica spent each evening curled up on Elizabeth's bed, reading magazines and gossiping while Elizabeth sat at her desk, trying to concentrate on her homework.

And, as each day passed, Elizabeth grew a little bit more upset about the way Amy was ordering her around. Amy couldn't seem to do *anything* for herself! At home, all Elizabeth heard was "Elizabeth, pick up my pencil," and "Elizabeth, I can't reach the light." Elizabeth, do this, Elizabeth do that—Elizabeth was almost ready to scream.

But the hardest of all to handle was the fact that, except for giving Elizabeth orders, Amy seemed to be doing her best to avoid her. Whenever Elizabeth tried to start a conversation, Amy suddenly remembered something pressing she had to do. At school, she had been hanging around with Jessica and the other Unicorns, who all treated her like an honorary member of the club. And for the past two days, Amy had eaten lunch with them at the Unicorner. *She might as well be a Unicorn*, Elizabeth thought glumly.

This Thursday was Locker Clean-out Day, the day when everybody was supposed to clean out his or her locker and to throw away all old papers and junk. Elizabeth cleaned hers before lunch, and then got a sandwich and joined Julie Porter and Sophia Rizzo. Amy was eating with the Unicorns.

Julie looked in Amy's direction. "Wouldn't you think that the Unicorns would be bored with Amy's story by now?"

Sophia nodded. "Brooke's party must not be giving them enough to talk about. Otherwise, they'd be sick and tired of hearing Amy tell about how she jumped out of her window and missed the net."

Elizabeth looked up from her sandwich. At first she thought Sophia was joking, and then she realized that she wasn't. "Missed the net?"

"And about how the ambulance almost crashed when it ran the red light," Julie added.

"And about how the doctor said that Amy's broken arm was the worst he'd seen in thirty years of broken arms," Sophia went on.

Elizabeth stared at her friends. "Wreck? Worst break? What are you talking about?"

Sophia frowned. "You know, Elizabeth. Amy

broke her arm when the smoke and flames forced her to jump out the window."

"Right," Julie agreed. "And the ambulance driver was going so fast that he skidded through a red light and nearly wiped out another car."

"Hasn't Amy told you any of this?" Sophia asked, looking a bit puzzled.

"Not exactly," Elizabeth answered slowly. "Is that what Amy has been telling everyone?"

Julie and Sophia exchanged a curious glance. "Yes," Julie said slowly. "You mean, things didn't happen the way Amy said they did?"

Suddenly, Elizabeth understood why Amy had refused to do the interview with her, and why she was going out of her way not to talk to her. She had exaggerated the story about the fire and she didn't want to admit it.

And if Amy was exaggerating the facts and embellishing the details when she talked to people, what would she write in her *Sixers* story? Would she tell the truth, or would she expect the *Sixers* to print a bunch of lies?

"What *is* it, Elizabeth?" Sophia asked, concerned.

Elizabeth sat there silently. The Amy who had always been her friend was not the kind of person who would deliberately deceive other people. She was not the kind of person who would hang around with the Unicorns, either, or put off working on an important science project, or waste her eve-

nings chattering about clothes and boys. The fire
had definitely changed Amy's personality, and not
for the better. Still, that was no reason for Elizabeth to hurt Amy by revealing the truth before she
was ready to do it herself.

"I'm not really sure what's going on," Elizabeth said finally. "I'd rather not talk about it until
I've talked to Amy."

"Looks like you'll have your chance right now,"
Julie said in a low voice. "Here she comes."

Amy stopped beside the table. "I wondered if
you'd give me a hand with my locker, Elizabeth.
With this cast, I can't clean it out by myself."

"Can't the *Unicorns* help you?" Julie asked,
lifting her chin.

"They're all busy," Amy said shortly. "I'm in
a hurry, Elizabeth."

Elizabeth looked down at her sandwich. "I'll
help you in a few minutes," she said. "After I've
finished my lunch."

Amy frowned. "My locker's pretty messy. If
we waste any more time, you won't be able to
clean it out before the bell rings for the next period."

"Amy," Sophia said mildly, "don't you think
you're being just a little bossy?"

Amy stared at her.

"Sophia's right, Amy," Julie said quietly. "Elizabeth isn't your slave, you know."

Elizabeth gulped down the last bite of her
sandwich. The last thing she wanted was for her

friends to get into a big argument. "It's OK," she said, getting up from the table. "I'm finished with my lunch."

Amy glanced down at Sophia and Julie. "Well," she said coldly, "I guess I know who my *friends* are. Come on, Elizabeth." Amy marched off, while Sophia and Julia looked on angrily.

As she walked off after Amy, Elizabeth wasn't sure that she would have enough patience and understanding to finish out the day, let alone the week.

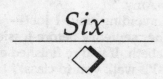

Six

Elizabeth pulled an untidy stack of papers from the bottom of Amy's locker. "Do you need to keep these?" she asked.

"Put them back," Amy said rudely. "It's old math homework. I might need it."

Elizabeth put the papers back and stood up. She had had just about enough of being ordered around. "Amy," she said firmly, "we need to talk."

Amy looked away. "What about?"

"About . . ." Elizabeth hesitated. "Well, about everything." It was getting terribly uncomfortable feeling so much confusion and resentment without letting Amy know how she felt. The truth about the fire had to be straightened out before Amy wrote her *Sixers* story. And Amy had to get serious about the science project, too. It was Thursday already, and they hadn't even started to work.

Amy looked at her watch. "The bell's going to ring in a few minutes," she said. "We'll have to talk later."

"When?" Elizabeth pressed. "You've been avoiding me, Amy."

"I'm *not* avoiding you. I just—" Amy didn't get to finish her sentence before Jessica appeared.

"Hi, Elizabeth. If you're finished cleaning your locker, Amy, I'll walk you to class."

"Sure, Jessica," Amy answered, sounding relieved. The two girls headed down the hall, leaving Elizabeth standing alone by the locker, feeling even more angry and resentful.

By that evening, Elizabeth was *really* ready for a talk. Amy had excused herself immediately after dinner, with the excuse that she had to work on her *Sixers* story. When Elizabeth went upstairs not long afterwards, she found Amy sitting at the desk, her face buried in her arms. She was crying.

"What's wrong, Amy?" Elizabeth exclaimed, bending over her. "Is your arm bothering you?"

Amy raised her head and wiped away a tear. "I just talked to Mom on the phone," she said. "She and Dad aren't having any luck at all finding a new house. They can't say how long I'm going to have to stay here."

"I'm sorry, Amy," Elizabeth replied sympathetically. "I really hope your folks will find a house soon."

"I'll bet you do," Amy burst out angrily. "The sooner they find someplace for us to live, the sooner you can get rid of me."

Elizabeth was shocked. "Amy! I don't want to get rid of you. I just want you to be happy, that's all."

Amy's face grew red as she forgot her sadness for anger. "I won't be happy until I have a home of my own to live in! I'm sick of having to share a room and wear borrowed clothes!"

Elizabeth was about to retort that she was getting pretty tired of sharing a room herself, when her mother appeared at the door.

"Before you two settle down to your homework," Mrs. Wakefield said cheerfully, "I think you ought to spend a few minutes tidying up your bathroom. There's a pile of wet towels on the floor and the sink needs cleaning." She glanced around at Elizabeth's messy room. "And it looks as if this room could stand some work, too."

Elizabeth glanced quickly at Amy, wondering if she would offer to help. But Amy only shrugged. "I'd be glad to help if I could, Mrs. Wakefield," she said apologetically. "But with this cast, I'm afraid I'm not much good. It's all I can do to write this story for the newspaper, and I have to turn it in tomorrow."

"I'll take care of the bathroom, and the mess in here, Mom," Elizabeth said. Slowly she went into the bathroom and shut the door so that she wouldn't have to hear any more of Amy's excuses. But she couldn't shut out the questions that kept circling around in her head. Why was Amy acting so selfishly? What was she writing in her *Sixers* article? And what was Elizabeth going to do if Amy turned in a story that wasn't factual?

Amy was feeling even more confused and upset than Elizabeth. She felt terribly guilty about the stupid lies she had told the kids at school, but she didn't see how she could possibly tell the truth now without making everybody hate her. She had tried to write her *Sixers* story in a way that didn't exactly reveal the whole embarrassing truth. But finally, after tearing up a half-dozen bad starts, she'd given up and had written the story pretty much the way she'd been telling it.

Amy was feeling even guiltier about the way she had been treating Elizabeth. She didn't intend to say such mean things to her, but they just kept popping out.

But what Amy felt guiltiest of all about was the fire itself. If only she'd taken the ashes out to the trash bin, instead of leaving them in the paper bag on the carpet. Then the fire would never have started and she wouldn't have had to tell such big lies, and she would still be friends with Elizabeth!

In fact, the only bright spot in Amy's life right now was her popularity with the Unicorns.

* * *

"You look very cute today, Amy," Lila said with an approving nod before homeroom on Friday. "I like that lavender blouse."

"Don't you think her hair looks good this way?" Jessica asked. Jessica had pulled Amy's blond hair into one ponytail over her right ear and tied it with a lavender ribbon.

"It really does," Lila replied. "I must say, Jessica, there's been quite a change in Amy's appearance—for the better. I just hope it lasts. I mean, I hope that all your good work isn't wasted, the way it was on Elizabeth."

Amy squirmed. It was nice of the Unicorns to loan her clothes and to pay her compliments, even if they sometimes talked about her as if she weren't present. But she *hated* the way they made fun of Elizabeth. That was nothing new, of course. The Unicorns had been doing that all year. It was just that Amy hadn't been around to hear them.

"Yes," Ellen said in a superior tone, fluffing her brown hair. "Whatever happened to the makeover you gave Elizabeth a few weeks ago, Jessica?"

"I guess she decided she didn't like it," Jessica said carelessly. "Oh, I forgot something in my locker. I have to get it before the bell rings. I'll see you guys later."

When Jessica had left the classroom, Lila and Ellen resumed their gossip about Elizabeth, who was standing by the blackboard, talking to Todd Wilkins.

"Just *look* at her," Lila said, wrinkling her nose. "She's wearing another one of those childish plaid blouses. I can't imagine what Todd sees in her."

"And she's wearing jeans and sneakers too," Ellen added. "She looks *so* immature. Doesn't she realize that she's growing up, or is she going to act like a baby forever?"

Amy felt her face getting red. She wished that she could make Lila and Ellen stop finding fault with Elizabeth. But if she said anything, they'd probably stop paying any attention to her. And Amy was afraid of losing anything, or anyone else right now.

Suddenly Ellen turned to Amy. "Don't *you* think that Elizabeth dresses like a baby?" Amy knew that the question was meant as a challenge.

Amy hesitated. "I . . . guess." She hesitated, giggled nervously. "Sometimes, maybe."

"She acts like a baby too," Ellen said scornfully. "I'll bet she even sleeps with a doll."

"Actually, it's a stuffed koala bear." The second the words had passed her lips, Amy regretted them. What had she done?

"A stuffed koala bear?" Lila shook her head in disbelief. "You've *got* to be kidding! People *our* age don't *do* things like that."

Ellen laughed. "I can't believe it. Elizabeth really sleeps with a stuffed bear?"

Amy swallowed hard. She wished she could sink into the ground. "I don't think she does it very often," she said hastily. "Actually, I've only seen her do it once."

"Once is enough," Ellen said nastily.

"But lots of kids collect stuffed toys," Amy objected.

"But they don't *sleep* with them." Lila snickered. "Not when they get to middle school, anyway. That's something only *babies* do."

"I guess that proves it," Ellen said, triumphantly. "Elizabeth is every bit as immature as we always said she was."

No, she isn't! Amy wanted to cry out. But she couldn't say a word. It was too late. Of all the stupid, mean things she had done in the past few days, this was the meanest and stupidest.

Elizabeth and Julie were standing outside the library after lunch on Friday, waiting for it to re-open. Two of the seventh-grade Unicorns passed them and giggled.

Elizabeth felt strangely uncomfortable. "Julie," she said, "have you noticed anything weird?"

"Weird how?" Julie asked.

"Those girls—they were giggling."

"There's nothing weird about that," Julie said. "Maybe they're passing around a new joke."

"It's just that I get the feeling that they're laughing at *me*." Elizabeth couldn't help remembering how awful she had felt when the Unicorns had started the rumor that she was looking for a boyfriend. That ridiculous rumor wasn't going around again, was it?

Just then Sophia came up, carrying a couple of library books. "Hi, Julie." Sophia glanced uneasily at Elizabeth. "Could I talk to you for a minute, Elizabeth?"

"Sure. What's up?" Elizabeth wanted to know.

Sophia looked apologetically at Julie. "Alone, I mean. Is that OK with you, Julie? We'll only be a minute."

Julie grinned. "Sure. As long as you're not going to talk about *me*. Anyway, the library's opening now. I'll go in and get a table for us, Elizabeth."

After Julie left, Sophia cleared her throat nervously. "I've just heard something, and I thought maybe you ought to know about it—if you don't already know."

"Know what?"

"Well," Sophia began, "it's about—"

At that moment, Bruce Patman walked by them. According to Jessica and the Unicorns, Bruce was the cutest boy in seventh grade. Elizabeth and her friends considered Bruce a bully, and just about as snobbish and selfish as Lila Fowler.

"Hi, Elizabeth." Bruce grinned. "Or should I call you Baby Bear?"

Elizabeth frowned. "What did you say?" she asked.

"I said, 'Hi, Baby Bear,' " Bruce replied mockingly. He turned around to Jerry McAllister, a sixth grader, who was almost as big a bully as Bruce.

"Baby Bear," Bruce repeated. "Hey, Jerry, don't you think that's a good nickname for Elizabeth?"

Jerry laughed loudly. "Baby Bear! Yeah, Bruce, that's pretty good, all right. Baby Bear!" Then he stuck his thumb in his mouth, crossed his eyes and made a funny face at Elizabeth.

"But I don't understand," Elizabeth said, her face growing flushed. "Why—?"

Bruce poked Jerry with his elbow. "Come on, Jerry. We don't want to be seen hanging around with the kindergarten crowd, do we?"

"You bet we don't. People might think we've been hired as babysitters." Jerry waggled his hand. "Bye-bye, Baby Bear."

"That was what I wanted to tell you about," Sophia said unhappily, as the boys went off down the hall. "The Unicorns are saying that you sleep with a stuffed bear. They're calling you a baby."

Elizabeth felt miserable. Did Jessica know that she sometimes slept with her old koala bear? Could she have told? *No*, Elizabeth told herself. Even if Jessica did know, she would *never* have betrayed Elizabeth that way.

But somebody else did know about the bear. Someone else had told the Unicorns.

That someone else had to be Amy.

Seven

◇

All that long afternoon, Bruce Patman and his friends went out of their way to make Elizabeth miserable. They stuck their thumbs in their mouths when she passed by in the hallway. Charlie Cashman yelled "Hi, Baby Bear" when he saw her standing beside her locker. And Dennis Cookman asked with mock concern if it wasn't time for her to take her afternoon nap.

Nora Mercandy and Julie caught up with Elizabeth after social studies class.

"I just heard, Elizabeth," Nora said, flipping her long black hair over her shoulders. "What a dumb thing for those guys to be saying! But I suppose they heard it from the Unicorns."

Elizabeth nodded. Nora herself had once been

the victim of Unicorn rumors. She probably understood just how Elizabeth felt.

"I can't imagine how such a ridiculous story got started," Julie said.

"It isn't ridiculous," Elizabeth said. "It's true. Once in a while, when I'm feeling really lonely or hurt, I sleep with my koala bear. I'm not ashamed of it," she added, straightening her shoulders. "If people want to laugh, then let them."

"But who could have told the Unicorns something as private as that?" Nora asked. "Was it Jessica?" Suddenly her dark eyes widened. "It wasn't *Amy*, was it? She's been hanging around with the Unicorns an awful lot lately."

Julie frowned. "Amy wouldn't do a thing like that. She's Elizabeth's best friend." She looked closely at Elizabeth. "It *wasn't* Amy, was it, Elizabeth?"

"Thanks for the sympathy," Elizabeth answered. "It's nice to have real friends." Then she walked away.

At first, Elizabeth had been terribly hurt by the boys' teasing, and by Amy's betrayal. But as the afternoon wore on, she had stopped feeling so hurt and had begun to feel very angry. Amy had done a lot of stupid things in the past few days, such as telling the Unicorns a lot of lies about the fire and about how she had broken her arm. But this was the most stupid and hurtful thing of all. And this time, Elizabeth vowed, she wasn't going to make any excuses for Amy. It didn't matter that she had a broken arm or that she had lost everything in the fire. Amy was going to own up to what she had done. She was going to apologize—or else!

Elizabeth kept her eye open for Amy. But every time she spotted her, Amy was with a group of Unicorns, giggling and whispering. And Elizabeth had a pretty good idea who they were whispering about.

Finally, Elizabeth thought of a place where she could talk to Amy alone. Today was the day that Amy was supposed to turn in her story about the fire. So after school, Elizabeth went to the *Sixers* room to wait.

"Hello, Elizabeth," Mr. Bowman said when she came in. "I'm glad you're here. I have to go to the principal's office for a few minutes and I'm expecting Amy to come by to hand in her story. Would you mind collecting it?"

"I wouldn't mind a bit," Elizabeth said grimly.

A few minutes after Mr. Bowman had left, Amy came in, her story in her hand. "Where's Mr. Bowman?" she demanded. "I have to turn something in."

Elizabeth folded her arms. "He's at the principal's office. Amy, I want to talk to you."

"I don't have time right now, Elizabeth," Amy answered uneasily. "Some kids are waiting for me."

"Some *Unicorns*, you mean." Elizabeth's blue-green eyes were flashing.

"Well, what about it?" Amy shot back. "What's wrong with the Unicorns? Just because they don't happen to like *you* very much—"

"I don't care whether the Unicorns like me or not," Elizabeth retorted icily. "But I do have a right to get upset when I hear that they're spreading stories about me. A story that they could have only heard from *you*."

"Story?" Amy asked nervously. "I don't know what you're talking about."

"Yes, you do," Elizabeth contradicted. "You told the Unicorns about my koala bear."

"That was no story," Amy muttered. "It was the truth." She looked away. "I have a right to tell the truth, don't I?"

"Not when you're telling it just to hurt somebody," Elizabeth said angrily. "And since when did *you* start worrying about the truth? That stuff you've been telling the Unicorns about the fire— you *know* it's all a lie! You didn't jump out of a window. You told me that you broke your arm when you tripped over your shoelace. I'll bet all that stuff about the ambulance running the red light and nearly getting into a wreck is a lie, too."

"That's enough, Elizabeth," Amy shouted. "I don't have to stand here and listen to this one minute longer!"

"Yes, you do!" Elizabeth shouted back. "You're going to listen while I tell you exactly what I think about the way you've been acting lately, hanging around with the Unicorns, ignoring me, Julie, and Sophia, acting like a slob—"

"A *slob*!" Amy screamed.

"That's *right*!" Elizabeth screamed back. "Ever since you moved in, my room's been a disaster area."

"Don't you two think," Mr. Bowman said from the doorway, "that you ought to have this kind of discussion outdoors? I could hear you halfway down the hall calling one another names."

Elizabeth felt her face flame. *Slob* was the very worst name she had ever called anybody. And she'd used it on her best friend, in front of her favorite teacher. "I'm sorry, Mr. Bowman," she muttered.

Without a word, Amy thrust her story into Mr. Bowman's hands and fled.

"It's not like you and Amy to yell at one another that way," Mr. Bowman said. "I thought you two were close friends."

"We were," Elizabeth said miserably. "But she's changed since the fire and I don't know what to do about it."

For a minute or two there was silence, as Mr. Bowman scanned Amy's story. When he had finished, he shook his head sympathetically. "Well, I'm not surprised that she's changed. Poor kid.

She went through a tragic ordeal. Just look at this." He handed Elizabeth Amy's story. "It sounds as if Amy's lucky that she got out of that house alive. But it's a terrific story. Front page material, I'd say."

Elizabeth took Amy's story and began to read. It was headlined "A Narrow Escape," and it contained the whole story—the story Amy had been telling the Unicorns, that is. Every single phony detail.

"Well?" Mr. Bowman asked. "It's a pretty thrilling account, don't you think? Highly dramatic. Our readers ought to really enjoy it."

Elizabeth nodded miserably. "Yes, it's thrilling all right." The trouble was that it wasn't *true*. Now Elizabeth was really in a fix. Should she tell Mr. Bowman that Amy's account was dishonest? Or should she just be quiet and let the *Sixers* print it?

"I see that there are a few spelling errors, and we can't work easily from a handwritten copy. Would you mind typing this for Amy, Elizabeth? You've got some time—we don't actually need it until next Tuesday, when we start putting the next issue together."

"I wouldn't mind." Elizabeth was relieved. At least she didn't have to decide what to do right away. Maybe over the weekend she could talk some sense into Amy and get her to rewrite the story. But Amy was so stubborn—she hated to be beaten. And admitting that she had lied was as good as being beaten.

"May I have some more macaroni salad, Elizabeth?" Amy asked politely that night at dinner.

"Here you are, Amy," Elizabeth replied, putting the salad on Amy's plate, her voice cold and proper.

Mrs. Wakefield raised her eyebrows and looked from Amy to Elizabeth. "How was school today?" she asked.

"It was fine, thank you," Amy said, looking directly at Mrs. Wakefield.

"It was terrific," Jessica blurted out. "Ellen has definitely talked Brooke Dennis into having a party next weekend. The Unicorns are going to help with the decorating."

"I thought your mother just finished decorating that house," Mr. Wakefield said teasingly.

Mrs. Wakefield smiled. "I think Jessica means *party* decorations. But I don't think that Ellen had much to do with the decision to have a party, Jessica. Mr. Dennis told me about it this afternoon. It's his party, too, and we're all invited."

"*Lots* of people are going to be invited," Jessica went on excitedly. "Ellen said that Mr. Dennis might even invite the cast of *Car Capers!*"

"Awesome!" Steven exclaimed.

Elizabeth was glad that Jessica had taken charge of the conversation. Right now, she couldn't think of anything but her argument with Amy and the predicament she was in about Amy's newspaper story.

For a while after dinner, Elizabeth tried to watch television, but she couldn't concentrate. Finally she went upstairs. In the hall, she bumped into Amy, her arms full of the clothes she had borrowed from the Unicorns. Elizabeth noticed that she was managing to carry them very well, even with her cast.

"What are you doing?"

"I'm moving my things into Jessica's room," Amy replied haughtily.

"Jessica's room!" Elizabeth exclaimed.

Amy raised her chin. "Jessica doesn't think that I'm a slob."

Elizabeth sighed. "I'm sorry for saying that, Amy. I guess I just lost my temper because of what you told the Unicorns."

"Well, if you think I'm going to apologize for a little thing like that, you're wrong! I don't have to apologize for telling the truth."

"Maybe not," Elizabeth replied calmly. "But you may have to apologize for *not* telling the truth."

Amy narrowed her blue-grey eyes. "What are you talking about, Elizabeth?"

"I'm talking about the story you wrote for the *Sixers*."

Amy hesitated, and a guilty look flashed across her face. Then she straightened her shoulders.

"My word is as good as yours, Elizabeth. Better, in fact. You weren't at the fire. *I* was." She paused. "Anyway, what harm is there in telling the story my way?"

Elizabeth stared at Amy. She wanted to point out that the truth was the *truth*, but she didn't think that Amy was in any mood for listening to anything she said right now. Instead, she asked, "What about our science project? We really have to get started on it, Amy, or we'll never get it finished by Tuesday."

Amy shook her head. "I've got my own ideas about the project. I'll get it done this weekend."

Elizabeth tried to respond, but she couldn't. The lump in her throat was too big. She and Amy had been friends as far back as she could remember. She couldn't believe that things between them had gone so wrong, so fast.

Elizabeth walked into her room and sat down heavily on her bed. After a moment, Jessica came in. Elizabeth could tell by the look on her face that she was furious.

"I've been humiliated, Elizabeth," Jessica cried dramatically. "And it's all your fault."

"*My* fault?" Elizabeth asked in surprise. "What are you talking about, Jess?"

Jessica folded her arms across her chest. "I'm talking about 'Baby Bear,' that's what."

Elizabeth sighed. "Oh, that. I wish you hadn't brought it up, Jessica. I've been trying to forget about it."

"Well, I wish I could forget about it!" Jessica cried. "But I can't! It's going to absolutely *ruin* my life—forever!"

"But what's all that silly stuff got to do with you?"

"Bruce Patman just phoned," Jessica said. "He was with Aaron Dallas and Jake Hamilton. And right in front of them, he called *me* Baby Bear. What's worse, he asked me if I sucked my thumb, too." She covered her face with her hands. "I'm *so* humiliated! And it's *your* fault, Elizabeth!"

Elizabeth usually found Jessica's theatrical behavior amusing. But tonight she was in no mood for it.

"Well," she said angrily, "if your good friends the Unicorns hadn't been so quick to tell Bruce Patman about my bear, he wouldn't be teasing you."

Jessica dropped her hands. "If your friend Amy hadn't seen you sleeping with your bear, the Unicorns wouldn't have had anything to tell."

"Amy isn't my friend," Elizabeth replied unhappily.

"Well, she told me that she didn't actually mean to tell about the bear. It just sort of slipped out. But you're right about her not being your friend anymore. She'd rather stay with me than with you. *I* don't call her names." And with that, Jessica marched out and slammed the door behind her.

For the first time since Amy had moved in, Elizabeth broke down and cried. It had been the most awful day of her life. She had been teased and tormented by the boys at school. She had gotten into a terrible fight with Amy and their friendship was destroyed—maybe forever. And now Jessica was mad at her over something that wasn't even her fault. Elizabeth had never felt so alone.

Amy was shoving her borrowed clothes into Jessica's closet. She had just finished talking to her mother on the phone. Her parents still hadn't found a place for them to live. But Mrs. Sutton had said that it was time Amy got some new clothes of her own. She was going to stop at the Wakefields' in the morning and leave some money for Amy. As far as Amy was concerned, nothing could have made her happier. She was getting pretty tired of wearing purple.

Behind her, Jessica was still complaining bitterly about what Bruce Patman had said to her and about the fact that Aaron Dallas had heard him say it.

"I wish Bruce Patman would keep his mouth shut," Jessica said furiously.

"Why don't you tell him off?" Amy asked. She'd been only half listening to Jessica's complaints. She was still thinking about Elizabeth, and feeling worse by the minute. Elizabeth had called her a slob, and she was right. Elizabeth was right about the lies, too. And about the bear. If only she hadn't told the Unicorns about Elizabeth's bear! If only there was some way to make it up to Elizabeth.

"Nobody tells Bruce off," Jessica said, horrified.

"Well, I guess you'll have to put up with it, then." Amy turned back to the closet with Tamara's purple top.

"You don't think it will make any difference to Aaron, do you, Amy?" Jessica asked anxiously.

"Probably not," Amy replied, trying to keep her patience. "If Aaron really likes you, he won't care what Bruce says."

"The trouble is," Jessica fretted, almost as if Amy hadn't spoken, "that once Bruce starts on something, it's almost impossible to get him to stop. Pretty soon, Lila and Ellen will hear what he's saying. Maybe they already have! I'll be a social outcast!"

"Jessica," Amy said impatiently, "if Lila and Ellen are your friends, you don't have to worry. They'll like you *anyway*, no matter what people say."

To tell the truth, Amy was getting just a little tired of the way Jessica was behaving. She was acting as if her whole reputation had suffered from what that stupid Bruce Patman had said to her. As far as Amy was concerned, Jessica was making a lot of fuss over nothing.

"This whole thing is Elizabeth's fault," Jessica said, frowning. "If she hadn't slept with that stupid old bear, none of this would have happened."

Amy sighed unhappily. She knew that it wasn't Elizabeth's fault. She knew that it was *her* fault, for having told the Unicorns. And when the Unicorns had told Bruce, the story had gotten completely out of control.

Amy could feel the tears pricking at her eyelids. The story about the fire had started that way, too. She hadn't meant to lie. She just hadn't wanted to tell people that she'd broken her arm when she tripped over her shoelace. Then, when it had come to the *Sixers* story, she had to write things the same way she'd told them, or confess that she'd been lying and look like an idiot in front of the Unicorns and everybody else. Amy blinked her eyes, trying to keep back her tears. She couldn't believe what a horrible mess she'd made out of things.

"Amy, are you crying?"

"Not really," Amy replied, wiping her eyes with the back of her hand.

Jessica sniffed. "Well, if you're feeling guilty over that business about the bear, I think you ought to stop. You've already told me that you didn't *mean* to let it slip out. It was an accident. Nobody can blame you for it." Jessica leapt off her bed. "Tell you what. I'll call Lila and Ellen and tell them that you're going shopping tomorrow. Maybe they'd like to go with us. Does that make you feel a little better?"

It didn't make Amy feel better at all. Amy only cried harder. She hadn't *meant* to do any of it—to tell lies, to hurt Elizabeth.

Most of all, she hadn't meant to start the fire.

Elizabeth was just wiping her eyes when her mother peeked through the door of the bedroom.

"Elizabeth," she said, "would you and Amy like to make some fudge this evening?"

"You'll have to ask Amy," Elizabeth said sadly. "She's staying in Jessica's room now."

Mrs. Wakefield came in and sat down on the bed. "Have you and Amy had an argument?" she asked gently.

Elizabeth nodded.

"What happened?" Mrs. Wakefield looked around with a little smile at the mess Amy had left behind. "Was it her untidiness? Or the fact that she kept putting off the science project?"

"No," Elizabeth said. "Not really." She sniffled. "It was what she told the Unicorns. About my sleeping with my stuffed bear."

"Your koala bear?" Mrs. Wakefield asked. "I didn't know you still slept with it."

"I don't," Elizabeth replied. "At least, not very often. But I did the other night, and Amy saw it. She told Lila and Ellen, and they spread it all over school." She sniffled again. "Now everybody thinks that I'm a baby." She swallowed. "Bruce Patman called me Baby Bear."

"Baby Bear?" Mrs. Wakefield smiled. "Well, there *are* worse names to be called, Elizabeth." Then she leaned over and gave Elizabeth a hug. "But it's wrong to call someone a name. And Amy was wrong to have told the others a secret of yours."

"There are lots of other things that Amy shouldn't have told," Elizabeth said gloomily, and she related to her mother what had happened over the past several days. When she was done, Mrs. Wakefield's face was serious.

"It sounds as if Amy has had some problems adjusting to life after the fire," she said. "Maybe it made her feel better when people paid attention to her. When they began to treat her like a star, she just kept exaggerating."

"Exaggerating to the Unicorns isn't such a big deal," Elizabeth said. "Pretty soon they'll have something else on their minds. They'll forget all about the fire—and about Amy, too," she added unhappily. "They'll drop her."

"If you're right," Mrs. Wakefield said, "she's probably in for a big disappointment."

Elizabeth nodded. "I'm afraid she is going to be hurt. But that's Amy's problem. *My* problem is that she wrote all that false stuff about the fire in her *Sixers* story. If I can't get her to change it, I'll have to decide whether or not to tell Mr. Bowman. I've got to do something about my science project, too."

"When does the story have to be in?" Mrs. Wakefield asked.

"Not until Tuesday."

"Well, it's only Friday. By Tuesday, Amy may see that she's been wrong. Maybe she'll decide to rewrite the story herself."

"Maybe," Elizabeth said unhappily, "but I doubt it. Amy's pretty stubborn. She hates to admit that she's been wrong."

Mrs. Wakefield gave her daughter a sympathetic look. "I wish I had some magic words that would make everything all right again, Elizabeth. But I don't. This sounds like the kind of problem that will have to solve itself over time."

Elizabeth managed a smile. "Thanks for the talk."

Her mother smiled back. "Don't mention it. You know, the offer on the fudge is still open. How about we make it together? There's a good movie on TV a little later, and some fudge would make a great movie snack."

Elizabeth nodded and followed her mother to the kitchen. A plate of warm fudge and a good movie—maybe Friday wasn't going to be a total loss, after all.

Eight

◇

Elizabeth spent the whole night thinking about Amy's article, and by the next morning, she still hadn't decided what to do. Amy would be terribly embarrassed if Elizabeth had to tell Mr. Bowman the truth about the story and Elizabeth dreaded making the situation any more complicated than it already was. Elizabeth decided that until she could see her way clear of the entire mess, it would be better for everybody if she kept her worries to herself.

So on Saturday morning Elizabeth got up early, and put on her favorite red-checked blouse, a short denim skirt, and a pair of red sandals. She brushed her hair into a ponytail and tied it with a red ribbon. Then she went downstairs, made enough pancakes for the whole family, and put them in the oven to keep warm. She was pouring out glasses of juice when Jessica and Amy came downstairs.

"Good morning, Jessica," Elizabeth said cheerfully. "Good morning, Amy. That's a cute outfit you're wearing. I like that purple top."

"It belongs to Tamara," Amy said quietly.

Jessica seemed to have forgotten all about the argument she'd had with Elizabeth the night before. "On the phone yesterday, Amy's mother told her that she could buy some new clothes, so we're going shopping with Lila this morning." Her eyes sparkled. "We're going to get Amy a whole new wardrobe!"

"Well, not a *whole* new wardrobe," Amy said uncomfortably. "Mom said I could buy some new things now, like school clothes and pajamas and stuff. She wants to take me shopping with her next week to buy the rest of what I'll need."

"I'm sure you're tired of borrowed clothes," Elizabeth said, remembering Amy's bitter complaint. "You'll probably be glad to have your own things."

Amy smiled shyly. "I will."

"I talked to Lila on the phone last night, and she has some very good ideas about the kind of clothes Amy ought to have. I think it's nice of the Unicorns to be so interested, don't you?" Jessica said, helping herself to several pancakes and smothering them with syrup. "Afterwards, Amy, we can go to a movie at the mall. What do you think of that?"

Amy hesitated. "It's awfully nice of the Unicorns to offer to help me pick out some clothes. But I don't know about a movie. I really ought to spend some time today working on my science project."

"But it's not due until Tuesday," Jessica said reassuringly. "You've got plenty of time. You can work on it all day tomorrow, if you want."

"Well, OK, I guess," Amy said reluctantly.

"What are you going to do today, Elizabeth?" Jessica gulped the last of her orange juice.

"I'm going to the library to work on my science project," Elizabeth replied, careful not to look at Amy. "After that, Dad's going to help me make a model of a rain forest. He said I can use some of the trees from his old model railroad."

"That sounds like an interesting idea, Elizabeth," Amy said, also avoiding Elizabeth's eye.

The doorbell rang and Jessica pushed back her chair. "That's probably your mom with your shopping money. Come on, Amy."

Amy looked at the dirty dishes stacked on the counter. "I'd offer to help with the dishes, but I can't because of my cast."

"That's OK," Elizabeth said cheerfully. "There aren't very many. I can do them."

Amy and Jessica were already at the Fowler's big mansion when Ellen walked in with Brooke

Dennis. Brooke was a tall, pretty girl, with big brown eyes and soft brown curls. Brooke always wore fashionable but comfortable clothes. This morning she was wearing a pair of white pants and a lemon-yellow top, with matching yellow beads and a bracelet.

"I've brought Brooke along," Ellen announced importantly, "because we need to buy some decorations for her party. There's going to be one room set aside for kids only, and the Unicorns are in charge of it. After we buy the decorations, Brooke's invited us over to her house for a planning session."

Jessica frowned. On the phone last night, Ellen had told her that she definitely did not want to go shopping with them today. What was she trying to pull?

"Good morning, Brooke," Lila said graciously. "It's terrific of you to ask us to help with your party."

"I'm glad for the help," Brooke said with a warm smile. "And I'm glad that so many kids want to come. It's going to be a super party."

"Even more will want to come when they hear who's invited," Ellen bragged, as if the party were her own.

"Who?" Lila asked. "Don't keep us in suspense, Ellen!"

Jessica's frown deepened. She didn't like the way Ellen was trying to steal all of the attention. Not only was she taking all the credit for arranging Brooke's party, but she was trying to distract Lila from their shopping trip with Amy.

"The cast of *Car Capers*, that's who!" Ellen announced.

"Wow," Amy breathed.

"Of course," Brooke said, "we don't know yet whether they can all come."

"But they've been *invited*," Ellen emphasized. "Mr. Dennis is inviting a special band too." The look she gave Jessica was clearly triumphant. "Come on, let's go get the material for the decorations. We've got a *lot* to do."

"Wait a minute, Ellen," Jessica broke in. "Lila and I are going shopping with Amy this morning. We were just about to leave for the mall when you showed up."

"That's right, Ellen," Lila said with a little frown. "Did you forget?"

"Of course not. But you don't have to spend more than an hour shopping." Ellen replied. "Anyway, Brooke's party is next Friday, so we can't waste a minute." Ellen looked pointedly at Amy. "We really don't have time for a project that doesn't benefit *Unicorns*."

Brooke smiled at Amy. "It shouldn't take very long to choose the materials for the party decorations," she said. "Anyway, it's more important to help Amy with her shopping."

"Brooke's right," Jessica said. "We can buy Amy's clothes first, then get stuff for the party."

"Then it's settled," Lila said. "First, we concentrate on Amy's wardrobe, then on the party. I've got it all planned, Amy," she announced authoritatively as she produced a lengthy list. "You're going to need several very sophisticated party dresses, of course. They're top priority. And some pretty blouses and skirts for school, and a few pairs of pants."

"I don't know about the party dresses," Amy said timidly. "My mom said I shouldn't buy that kind of stuff until I need it. But I do need several pairs of jeans. That's what I usually wear to school. And some pajamas."

Ellen raised her eyebrows. "Jeans?" she asked disdainfully.

Lila wrinkled her nose. "I was thinking more of pants than of jeans, Amy. Pants like the pair that Brooke is wearing." She smiled approvingly at Brooke. "I really like your outfit, Brooke."

Amy shook her head. "Brooke's pants are cute, but they're white. I'd never be able to keep white pants clean."

Lila looked surprised, and Jessica stood up quickly. Jessica didn't like the way things were going. "Let's go, you guys," she said. "It's always easier for me to decide what clothes I need when I'm actually trying something on."

At the mall, Amy followed Jessica and the others as Lila led them straight to Valley Fashions.

Amy had never shopped there, but Lila assured her that it was *the* place to buy clothes.

"I never buy anywhere else," she said. "They have all the top designer labels."

Amy glanced at a price tag and gave a startled yelp. "Wow! They've got top prices, too! I can't afford this stuff." Her mother had given her what seemed like a lot of money, but it certainly wouldn't go very far in an expensive shop like this.

Lila arched her eyebrows. "Can't afford it?" She peered at the price tag that had shocked Amy. "Why, that's not very much, for an outfit with that label."

Ellen smiled sweetly. "Maybe Amy would rather try the discount store."

"What Amy means," Jessica explained hurriedly, "is that she'd like to buy one or two really good things here, like a few party dresses. Then she could buy the other things at—"

"But that isn't at all what I mean, Jessica," Amy interrupted. She looked around at the fancy designer clothes. "These things are much too expensive for my budget," she said. "And they're not my style, either."

Lila put her hands on her hips. "Well, then," she said distantly, "maybe you should tell us what store you had in mind."

Amy shifted from one foot to the other. She knew that Lila spent a great deal of money on designer outfits. She should have known that Lila was not the best person to help her shop for ordinary school clothes.

"Yes," Ellen said with an amused smile. "Tell us just where you want to shop, Amy."

"Let's go to Wilsons'," Amy said. Her mother had suggested that she shop there. It wasn't a discount store, but its clothes were reasonably priced.

"*Wilsons'*?" Lila cast a withering glance at Amy. "Well, I suppose, if you don't think you can afford anything here. But I must say—"

"Wilsons' has some really cute things," Amy interrupted. "And the prices are good, too."

"Jessica's right," Brooke said with a smile. "If Amy wants to shop there, why don't we get started."

"Well," Lila said, with one last regretful glance around Valley Fashions, "All right. If Brooke says so, I guess we'll go to Wilsons'," Lila headed for the door. "Come on. We don't have all day."

"That's right, Lila," Ellen agreed. "We have more important things to do. Like getting ready for Brooke's party."

Amy and the Unicorns spent the next hour shopping at Wilsons'. At first, Amy didn't really mind Lila's bossiness and fashion advice. But after a little bit, it began to grate on her nerves. And when Lila tried to get her to try on a dressy purple blouse with a fluffy ruffle down the front, Amy put her foot down.

"I don't like ruffles, and purple isn't my best color."

Lila looked distastefully at the casual yellow-print tee shirt that Amy had picked out instead. "I really don't think I can be of any further help here. Jessica, maybe you'd better stay with Amy. The rest of us will go to the paper goods store and start shopping for the party."

"Amy's almost finished, Lila," Jessica replied firmly.

"No, I'm not," Amy said. "I still have to get my jeans, and maybe a skirt." But with Lila out of the way, Amy's shopping didn't take very long and she found herself tagging after Jessica and the other Unicorns as they shopped for crepe paper, balloons, and paper flowers. Brooke chose the colors quickly, but Lila and Ellen and Jessica argued endlessly over exactly what and how much to get.

Amy quickly grew bored with standing around listening to the Unicorns argue over which shade of purple crepe paper they ought to buy. And she had noticed a difference in the way they were treating her. Of course, Ellen had never been friendly. But now she was making it clear that she thought that Amy had no place butting into Unicorn business. Lila, who had been very nice all week long, had suddenly become cool and distant. She was totally ignoring Amy and focusing all her attention on Brooke, laughing at her jokes and paying her lots of outrageous compliments.

Jessica was still being polite, but even she was paying more attention to Brooke than she was to Amy.

Jessica could see that trouble was brewing. Lila was beginning to turn very cool toward Amy, and Ellen was being nastier than she'd been all week. Even worse, she noticed that Amy was beginning to get jealous of the fact that Lila and Ellen were paying more attention to Brooke than to her. Several times, Amy had brought up the subject of the fire or her broken arm. But when no one had responded, she had turned sullen. She was being such a wet blanket that it really would be best if she went home. But if she did, Ellen would think that she had chased her off. Amy wasn't Jessica's favorite person, especially when she was acting so silly. But Jessica couldn't let Ellen win. After all, Amy *was* Jessica's house guest, and in a way, her protégé.

When they got to Brooke's house, Amy pulled Jessica aside.

"Jessica," she said in a low voice, "I don't want to hang around here anymore."

"Why?" Jessica asked. "We're having fun. We're going over to Lila's next to work on the decorations. There's a lot to do for the party. The whole Unicorn Club is planning to work all day tomorrow. And I want you to come and help."

"But I have to get started on my science project," Amy protested. "It's due on Tuesday."

Jessica shrugged. "You can ask Ms. Caxton to give you another week," she said, pointing to Amy's cast. "She can't turn you down. You've got a perfect excuse."

"I suppose," Amy said doubtfully.

"Then stop making such a big deal about it," Jessica commanded. "And stop looking so sad. For the past couple of hours, you've been acting as if you've lost your best friend."

"Maybe I have," Amy whispered.

Jessica ignored Amy's response and continued in a sterner tone. "Really, Amy, you ought to make more of an effort to be friendly."

"Friendly!" Amy exclaimed.

"Sssh," Jessica hissed. "Lila and Ellen will hear you."

Amy frowned indignantly. "What about Lila and Ellen being friendly with me? All day long they've been acting as if they don't want me around. Especially Ellen."

Jessica was beginning to get angry. "Listen, Amy. The Unicorns have gone out of their way to be friendly with you. They've eaten lunch with you all week. Lila was even happy to help you pick out your clothes—until you stuck up your nose at her ideas. The least you can do is be friendly."

"I'd rather go home," Amy insisted sullenly. "I mean, back to your house."

Jessica thought furiously. She knew that Amy and Ellen Riteman didn't like each other.

"If you leave," Jessica said, "Ellen will think that she chased you off. She'll tell everybody she got rid of you. Is that what you want?"

Amy squared her shoulders. "No."

"Then come on," Jessica ordered. "Ignore Ellen. And be friendly."

So Amy spent what to her was a totally boring and often painful Saturday and Sunday with the Unicorns. By Sunday evening, she was sick of trying to ignore Ellen and being friendly to a group of people who treated her like an outsider. But as much as she hated to admit it, now that she no longer had Elizabeth to turn to, she was afraid to lose the only friends she had left.

Nine

◇

Elizabeth had spent the entire weekend working on her science project. The rain forest model she had built with her father's help was much more complicated than the chart she and Amy had originally prepared. Elizabeth felt proud of her work, and glad that it was finished at last. She was glad of something else, too. While she had worked on her project, she had managed to forget all about the problem of Amy's *Sixers* story. She had also managed to forget about Bruce Patman and the Baby Bear episode.

But now it was Monday morning, and Elizabeth was dreading going to school. She just knew that the minute she walked in the door, one of

Bruce's buddies would yell out "Baby Bear!" It was going to be a horrible day.

When Elizabeth got to homeroom, the first person she saw was Caroline Pearce, who came running up to her.

Oh, no! Elizabeth thought, cringing. *What am I going to say if Caroline asks me about my koala bear?*

But Caroline had other things on her mind. "Have you heard the latest news about Brooke Dennis's party?" she demanded eagerly.

Elizabeth gave a sigh of relief. At least they weren't going to talk about last week's gossip. "I've heard that Mr. Dennis is inviting the cast of *Car Capers*," Elizabeth said.

"But there's more!" Caroline exclaimed excitedly. "Something even *more* terrific! Brooke's father has asked Dynamo to play for the party!"

"Dynamo?" Elizabeth asked, her eyes widening. Everybody at school was talking about Dynamo's latest music video, which was rapidly rising to the top of the charts. And every girl was wild over Nick England, the group's lead singer.

"That's right," Caroline said. "Confidentially, I heard that Mr. Dennis is an old friend of Nick England's. He even helped him to get started in the music business. So Nick England is paying back the favor."

"Well, I'm glad there's going to be such a big

party," Elizabeth laughed. "It'll give everybody something to look forward to."

And to talk about, she added to herself. She had a hunch that the silly story that had gone around about her on Friday would be forgotten in the new excitement.

Elizabeth's hunch turned out to be right. The entire school was buzzing about the Dennises' party. The party was going to be an indoor-outdoor event to show off both the grounds' new landscaping and the house's new styling. And Mrs. Wakefield had been right. Mr. Dennis's friends, as well as Brooke's friends, were invited. And just about every kid at Sweet Valley Middle School, including the seventh and eighth graders, was suddenly claiming to be Brooke's good friend.

Nobody cared about teasing Elizabeth anymore. Nobody cared about the Suttons' fire, or about Amy's broken arm.

"If you ask me," Julie Porter said to Elizabeth at lunch on Monday, "Amy has a problem."

Sophia Rizzo glanced toward the Unicorns' table. "I agree," she said, munching her sandwich. "Nobody's paying any attention to her."

Amy was sitting with Jessica and the Unicorns, as she had the previous week. But last week, she had sat in the middle of the long table, with Unicorns clustered around her and across from her. Now, she and Jessica were sitting at one end of the table, while Brooke Dennis sat in the middle, the object of the Unicorns' admiration. Each of the girls seemed to be trying to outdo the other to capture Brooke's attention.

"Poor Amy," Julie said, reaching for a potato chip. The Unicorns must be bored with her story. Now, they've got something more important to think about. They're all angling for invitations to Brooke's party. And they all want to be friends with somebody whose father is a friend of Nick England's."

"Well," Sophia said tartly, "Amy doesn't have to sit there and be ignored. She can always come over here and eat with her *real* friends."

"Maybe she doesn't think she can." Julie gave Elizabeth a sideways glance. "At least, not after the big argument she and Elizabeth had on Friday."

"Argument?" Sophia asked curiously.

Elizabeth put down her sandwich. "How did you find out about it?"

Julie gave her a sympathetic look. "I came down the hall when you guys were yelling at one another in the *Sixers* room. I was really surprised. I always thought you two were such good friends."

"We *were* good friends," Elizabeth said sadly. "But not anymore."

"But Amy's staying with you, isn't she?" Sophia asked.

"She's staying with *Jessica*," Elizabeth said. "She moved her stuff into Jessica's room on Friday night. I didn't see her all weekend. She was tied up with Jessica and the Unicorns."

Julie glanced back at Amy. "It doesn't look to me as if the Unicorns want her now. Why is she even bothering to hang around?"

"It's my guess that she's doing it to show them she *can*," Sophia said. "You know how stubborn Amy can be."

"That's silly," Julie said with a frown.

Elizabeth agreed. It was silly. But she also knew that there wasn't a thing she could do to help Amy handle the Unicorns. She had her own worries. She was still trying to decide what she was going to say to Mr. Bowman about the story Amy had written.

Over at the Unicorns' table, Amy couldn't remember when she had endured a more uncomfortable lunch period. Even Jessica was giving her the cold shoulder. But at last the Unicorns began to leave for the next class. Amy breathed a sigh of relief when Ellen got up. Now *she* could leave too, and nobody could say that Ellen had chased her off. She was getting tired of playing Ellen's silly game.

And Amy had other things to worry about. Her science project, for instance. She had let Jessica talk her into putting it off. But it was due tomorrow, and she was going to have to tell Ms. Caxton that it wasn't finished. Amy had decided that she would wait until after science class to speak with her. It would be too embarrassing if Elizabeth overheard her begging for more time.

But she didn't get a chance to speak in private. Amy had just gotten to the science classroom when Ms. Caxton came up to her.

"Good afternoon, Amy," she said. "How's your arm? Better, I hope?"

Amy put on a rather pained expression. "Well, to tell the truth, I–"

But before she could finish, Ms. Caxton had turned to Elizabeth who was sitting nearby. "Will you and Amy be ready with your project tomorrow, Elizabeth?"

Elizabeth looked up from her science book. "I'll be ready with mine," she said quietly.

Ms. Caxton frowned. "But I thought you and Amy were working together."

"We changed our minds," Elizabeth said. "Amy's doing her own project."

"Well, then, I'll look forward to seeing what you've come up with, Elizabeth," Ms. Caxton said cheerfully. She turned to Amy. "And, Amy, I'll look forward to yours, too."

Amy's mouth was dry. She glanced at Elizabeth, who had gotten up from her seat and gone to the bookshelf. "Um, I need to talk to you about that, Ms. Caxton."

"Is there a problem?" Ms. Caxton asked.

"Well, sort of," Amy confessed. "You see, I

just haven't been able to get the project done. It's *so* hard to work with this cast on. I'd like another few days, please. Could I turn it in next Monday?"

Ms. Caxton looked troubled. "But I've noticed that you're able to write in class without any difficulty, Amy." She shook her head. "No, I'm afraid that you've had plenty of time to get your project done. The deadline is still tomorrow. And don't forget about the oral quiz."

Feeling utterly hopeless and sorry for herself, Amy slumped down into her seat. If her project wasn't done by tomorrow, she'd get an F on the unit. How had she let Jessica get her into such a terrible predicament?

But it wasn't Jessica who had gotten her into this awful mess, Amy realized. She'd gotten into it herself. It wasn't just the science project, either. It was the stuff she had told the Unicorns and written in her *Sixers* story. It was her fight with Elizabeth. It was the fire and. . . . It was all one big, horrible mess of her own making.

For a moment Amy thought of running straight to the library after school to begin work on the project, but then she remembered that her mother was picking her up today to take her to the doctor. Although they'd talked on the phone, Amy had only seen her mother once briefly Saturday morning, and she'd been looking forward to spending the afternoon with her. But as the day dragged on, Amy became more and more worried about her science project, and her spirits sank lower and lower. By the time the final bell rang, Amy was sure that she couldn't feel any worse.

Amy's mother picked her up as planned and drove her to the doctor's office. After a brief exam, the doctor announced that her arm was healing well. So well, in fact, he thought she'd be ready for a smaller cast in another week.

"Your father and I are hoping we'll be able to find somewhere to live before long," Mrs. Sutton said, as they walked back to the car. "We have a few good leads."

"I hope so," Amy said fervently.

Her mother took her car keys out of her purse. "But I thought you'd enjoy staying at the Wakefields," she said with concern. "You and Elizabeth are always begging to spend the night together." She laughed. "Don't try to pull the wool over my eyes, Amy. I'll bet the last week has been one long slumber party for the two of you."

"Well, not exactly," Amy said quietly. "I'm not sleeping in Elizabeth's room. I moved in with Jessica."

"Jessica?" Mrs. Sutton asked, opening the car door. "That's a surprise. Oh, by the way, Amy, we're getting the report from the insurance company tomorrow. We may finally know what caused the fire."

"Oh." Amy felt the color drain from her face. "I didn't realize we would know so soon."

"I'll be glad when this whole thing is settled,"
Mrs. Sutton said. "It's hard to plan for the future
when you're not sure—"

"Why, hello, Amy. Hello, Mrs. Sutton." Mr.
Bowman was just getting out of his car which he
had parked next to theirs.

"Good afternoon, Mr. Bowman," Mrs. Sutton
said. "I'm glad to tell you that the doctor has
given Amy an 'A' on the way her arm is healing.
It wasn't a very bad break, and it's coming along
just fine."

"That's good to hear." Mr. Bowman shook
his head. "After the awful ordeal of the fire and
Amy's narrow escape, you must be glad to have
good news for a change. It could have been a
terrible tragedy."

"Mom," Amy said quickly, "I'm getting a little stomach ache. Do you think we could—"

Mrs. Sutton nodded. "It was dreadful to lose
the house and all our things," she said. "But it
wasn't exactly a narrow escape. Thankfully, we
had plenty of time to get out of the house." She
smiled fondly at Amy. "If Amy hadn't tripped on
her shoelace, she wouldn't even have broken her
arm."

Mr. Bowman frowned. "Her shoelace?"

"Yes," Mrs. Sutton said. "She tripped over
her shoelace running down the porch steps."

Mr. Bowman looked carefully at Amy. "But
what about the window?"

"The window?" Mrs. Sutton asked.

"*Mom*," Amy said urgently, "my stomach is *really* hurting. Couldn't we go?"

"I'm afraid I don't know what you're talking about, Mr. Bowman." Mrs. Sutton said politely.

Mr. Bowman hesitated for a moment. "It's nothing. Just a misunderstanding on my part."

"It's nice to have seen you."

"Nice to have seen you, too, Mrs. Sutton," Mr. Bowman replied. "Amy, I'm glad to hear that your arm is healing so well. Will you stop in and see me tomorrow? I'd like to talk to you about your story on the fire."

"Yes, sir," Amy said glumly, getting into the car.

"And I hope your stomach ache gets better," Mr. Bowman added with a little smile, as he turned to leave.

"You didn't tell me that you'd written a story for the newspaper, Amy," Mrs. Sutton said, as she buckled her seatbelt. "When will it come out?"

"In a couple of days," Amy said, almost in a whisper.

"You'll have to show it to me. I'd love to read it, and I know your father would, too. We could send a copy to Grandma Sutton."

Now Amy's stomach really *was* beginning to hurt.

*   *   *

Except for Amy, everybody around the Wakefield dinner table seemed to be excited about the Dennises' party on Friday. Because Mrs. Wakefield had decorated the Dennis house, the whole Wakefield family had been invited. Steven and Jessica were beside themselves with joy at the thought of actually getting to meet Nick England, as well as the cast of *Car Capers*. Mr. and Mrs. Wakefield knew that the party could be good publicity for Mrs. Wakefield's business, and Elizabeth was glad that the party had proved more exciting to the kids at school than her koala bear!

"It's the most important thing to happen in Sweet Valley in months and months!" Jessica said happily, passing the apple pie to Elizabeth. "*Everybody's* talking about it."

Mr. Wakefield grinned. "I'll bet Brooke's surprised by how many new friends she has."

"Maybe," Jessica said, putting a scoop of ice cream on top of her pie. "But she's spending so much time with the Unicorns that she really doesn't have time for anybody else."

"I'll bet," Steven said sarcastically, helping himself to another piece of pie. "I'll bet you, Lila, Janet, and Ellen have had her all sewed up."

Jessica gave him a haughty look. "Well, why not? We're her friends, aren't we?" She looked up at the clock. "In fact, I'm supposed to be over at Janet's right now, to work on paper flowers."

Elizabeth looked at Amy, noticing that most

of her dessert sat on her plate, untouched. She hadn't said anything all evening and was looking very glum.

"You're not going, Amy?" Elizabeth asked.

"No," Amy said quietly. Elizabeth thought she saw a look of relief on Jessica's face.

"Don't forget that it's your turn to help with the kitchen chores, Jessica," Mrs. Wakefield said.

"I'll be glad to take Jessica's place," Amy volunteered quickly.

Elizabeth and her mother were surprised. "Are you sure you can help in the kitchen with your cast?" Mrs. Wakefield asked.

Amy's face flushed. "I'm learning to manage better," she said, picking up her plate. "Anyway, the doctor said I could do just about anything I feel like doing. And I feel like helping."

"All right. But I think Jessica ought to give a hand, too. She's missed her turn for the past couple of days."

"But I need to be at Janet's," Jessica protested.

"I'll help too," Elizabeth said quickly. "That way, you can get out of the kitchen faster, Jess. And you can have the evening off, Mom."

Mrs. Wakefield grinned at Mr. Wakefield. "Since the girls are being so helpful, Ned, maybe it's a good night to take in that film we've been wanting to see."

"Brent Baines' new movie?" Jessica asked hopefully.

Mr. Wakefield laughed. "Definitely *not* Brent Baines' new movie. Come on, Alice. Let's get out of here while we've got the chance."

With the three girls working, it didn't take long to clear the table and wash the dishes. But Jessica kept looking at the clock and pointing out how late it was getting. Finally, Elizabeth ran out of patience.

"Jessica," she said, "we're almost finished. Why don't you go over to Janet's house?"

"I'm on my way," Jessica shouted, and headed for the door. "Bye, Elizabeth. Bye, Amy."

"Whew," Elizabeth said with a grin, as the door banged shut behind Jessica. "Why do I always think it's harder to do a job *with* Jessica than without her?"

Amy looked directly at her friend. "Elizabeth, I'm in terrible trouble. The very worst trouble of my life." And then she burst into tears.

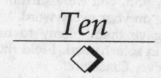

Ten

◆

Elizabeth put her arms around Amy and held her while she cried. Then, when the worst of the tears were over, she brought Amy a box of tissues.

"Tell me about it," Elizabeth said sympathetically. "If you want to, that is."

"Yes, I want to," Amy replied, wiping her eyes. "I've been wanting so badly to talk to you but I acted like such a jerk all last week. I was afraid you wouldn't want to hear what I have to tell you."

"What is it, Amy?" Elizabeth asked.

"The truth." Amy blew her nose. After a long silence, she began to speak in a very low voice. "It felt really great in the beginning, all of the attention the Unicorns were giving me. I felt so lost without my stuff, and so bad about the fire—having a lot of kids really interested in me made me feel less lonely. Everyone, especially the Unicorns, were almost begging me to exaggerate, to tell them something exciting. I guess everything sort of went to my head."

Elizabeth laughed. "You were a real star. Every time I saw you, you were surrounded by Unicorns hanging on your every word."

"And I gave them plenty to hang on to," Amy said. "I'm so ashamed. I told them stuff you wouldn't believe, Elizabeth."

"Like jumping out of the window?"

Amy blushed. "Thirty feet down. And breaking my arm when I jumped."

"And riding in an ambulance—"

"—that ran every stop light and nearly got in a wreck." Amy's blush deepened.

"And having the worst broken arm—"

"—that the doctor had ever seen in all his years of medical practice," Amy finished.

"It *does* make a very thrilling story, Amy."

"Yeah." Amy's face was flaming. "The trouble is, none of it is true."

"Don't worry. The Unicorns have forgotten all about the fire by now," Elizabeth said comfortingly. "They're so excited about Brooke's party that they can't think of anything else. In another week, they won't remember a word you said."

"That may be true," Amy said slowly. She

shook her head miserably. "But I did something worse than telling the Unicorns stuff that wasn't true. I wrote it all down for the whole school to read."

Elizabeth didn't reply and Amy went on.

"This is the really bad part. You know that interview you suggested for the *Sixers* story? Well, the reason I didn't want to do it was because I didn't want to face up to you after having told all those lies. And after having told a phony story, I couldn't figure out how to back out of it without looking like an idiot. So I wrote the story just the way I'd been telling it."

"I know," Elizabeth said quietly. "Mr. Bowman showed me the article."

Amy gulped. "He did? Then you can see why I'm in trouble. And what's more, my mother and I ran into Mr. Bowman today. While he was talking to my mother, he figured out that I'd exaggerated in my piece. He wants to see me tomorrow."

"Oh," Elizabeth said.

Amy's voice was hollow. "I don't know what to do. My mother wants to read it. She wants to show it to my father, too—and send it to my grandmother! I'm *doomed*, Elizabeth."

"No, you're not," Elizabeth replied firmly. "They're not going to read that story."

Amy's eyes widened. "They're not?"

"Nobody's going to read that story—at least, not before you rewrite it. That is, if you want to."

"I'd give anything to rewrite it!" Amy exclaimed. "But I've already handed it in to Mr. Bowman."

"He gave it to me Friday for some grammatical corrections," Elizabeth said. "It's upstairs on my desk."

"You're kidding!" Amy breathed incredulously.

"Would I kid about a thing like this?" Elizabeth gave Amy a close look. "You won't be embarrassed when you have to back down from what you've told everyone?"

Amy shook her head. "I'll be a lot worse than embarrassed if my parents find out about the lies I told. I'm nervous about facing Mr. Bowman, too. But it'll be easier to do once the story's rewritten."

"Maybe we can rewrite it in a way that avoids the problem," Elizabeth said thoughtfully. "We could write a straight news story, like the report on TV, and leave out all the gory details."

"Leave out the *thrilling* part, you mean?" Amy asked with a small smile.

Elizabeth grinned. "Right. For example, we could just say that you broke your arm leaving the house and were taken to the hospital in an ambulance. Maybe nobody will question your decision to write it that way."

Amy looked relieved. "Nobody that counts, anyway. And if you ask me, the Unicorns don't count."

"They seemed to count for plenty last week," Elizabeth remarked.

Amy sighed. "I really acted like a jerk, didn't I? And the worst part of it is that I knew it all the time, even though I didn't want to admit it."

"Knew what?" Elizabeth asked.

"I knew that they were just using me," Amy said. "That they didn't really *like* me. All they wanted was to be where the action was."

"Then why did you put up with it?"

"At first, it was because I needed to think that I was really special." Amy blushed. "After a while, though, I just got stubborn. I knew that the Unicorns, Ellen especially, didn't want me around, but I wasn't going to let them run me off."

Elizabeth nodded.

"I figure I don't have to apologize to the Unicorns for lying because I told them what they wanted to hear. But I do have to apologize to you for telling them about the stuffed bear, Elizabeth. That was a really rotten thing to do."

"I accept your apology," Elizabeth said. "But I think people have forgotten it by now. Bruce Patman didn't call me 'Baby Bear' once today."

Amy hung her head. "When I heard that, I really felt like a jerk."

"Brooke's party came along in the nick of time," Elizabeth said with a grin. "It gave everyone something to talk about besides my stuffed bear and your fire. It got us both off the hook."

Amy sighed dejectedly. "I'm not off the hook yet, believe me. For one thing, there's my science project. I spent so much time with the Unicorns that I didn't get a thing done on it this weekend. I asked Ms. Caxton for some extra time, but she said no. Tomorrow I'm going to get my first-ever F in science."

Elizabeth thought for a moment. "Why don't we tell Ms. Caxton that we changed our minds again and turn in a joint project? The rain forest model I made is mostly based on what we did together, before the fire. And I'll bet that if we go through my dad's old *National Geographic* magazines tonight, we can come up with enough pictures to make another chart, just like the first one. Then all we have to do is type up the report that goes with the chart and—"

Amy groaned. "You're making it sound so simple. But all that work will take *forever*."

"Only a few hours," Elizabeth said. "I've still got my notes from our other report."

"Your notes!" Amy exclaimed. "Liz, you're a lifesaver! Our project will be the best in the class!" Then her shoulders slumped. "I just wish you could do something about my *real* problem," she said sadly.

Elizabeth shook her head. "Your *real* problem? You mean the story you told the Unicorns, the stuff you wrote for the *Sixers*, and your science project—those aren't your *real* problem? Amy, what can be worse than that?"

Amy's eyes filled with tears. "Mom and Dad are going to get the insurance company's report tomorrow," she said in a choked voice. "They'll find out how the fire started."

"But I don't see what that has to do with—"

"They'll find out the *truth*, Elizabeth," Amy wailed. "They'll find out that *I'm* the one who started the fire!"

Elizabeth's heart nearly stopped. "You!"

"Me," Amy said miserably. "Remember, Sunday afternoon, when we were working on our project in the family room? It was chilly, and I lit a fire in the fireplace."

Elizabeth nodded. "I remember, but—"

"There were some old ashes in the fireplace. So before I lit the fire, I dumped a scoop of them in a paper bag. I meant to take it outside, but I forgot. When I went to bed, the bag was sitting there where I left it—on the carpet."

Elizabeth's eyes widened and she caught her breath. "So you think that there were some live embers in the ashes and the carpet caught fire?"

Amy nodded. A tear rolled down her cheek. "That's the only thing it could have been, Elizabeth."

"No," Elizabeth said firmly. "Sometimes fires start from faulty wiring or from the heating system. Anyway, you won't know for sure until tomorrow, when you hear the report."

"But I *can't* put it out of my mind!" Amy cried frantically. "When my parents get the report, they'll know that I'm responsible. And maybe when the insurance company finds out that I did it, they won't pay us." She began to sob. "We've lost our house and everything we own, Elizabeth, and it was *all my fault*! What will they *do* to me? And what will happen if the insurance company says it won't pay for our house and our stuff?"

Elizabeth's heart went out to Amy. What a terrible secret to carry around for a whole week! No wonder Amy hadn't acted like herself. No wonder she'd exaggerated the story about the fire and played up to the Unicorns to get their attention. No wonder she'd cried at night, when everyone else was asleep.

"It's OK, Amy," Elizabeth soothed, giving her friend another hug. "I know you feel awful. But crying isn't going to help. Let's go upstairs and get started on the science project and the *Sixers* story. And maybe the truth will turn out to be better than you think."

Amy wiped the tears from her eyes with the back of her hand. "Maybe," she said in an anguished voice. "But I wouldn't bet on it, Elizabeth."

The girls worked until after ten on their science project. It was easy to put together the chart from all the pictures they found in three or four magazines. It took longer to write the report but they shared the work. Elizabeth pulled out her electric typewriter and typed what Amy read to her from the notes.

When they had finally completed the science project, they turned to Amy's *Sixers* story. Amy groaned when she reread it. "I can't *believe* I wrote this awful stuff! Who was I trying to fool?"

"The Unicorns?" Elizabeth laughed. "If you ask me, they had it coming."

A half hour later, the story was also finished and neatly typed up, and the girls got into their pajamas.

"Want me to help you?" Elizabeth asked.

"Thanks," Amy said. "I think I can manage." When she was brushing her teeth a while later, Elizabeth noticed that Amy had neatly folded the bathroom towels and cleaned out the basin.

Ms. Caxton was surprised and pleased when Elizabeth and Amy brought in their joint science project. "You've done a great deal of work," she said when they showed her the chart and the model rain forest. "Are you ready for your oral quiz?"

Both girls nodded tensely. And, as usual, they each got an A.

"Well, that's over," Amy said with a sigh of relief, as they walked out of the classroom. "Now I can worry about facing Mr. Bowman!"

"Do you want me to come with you?" Elizabeth asked.

Amy shook her head. "Thanks, Elizabeth. But I'm the one who made up the lies. I think I ought to be the one to tell the truth."

"Good luck," Elizabeth said with a smile.

Mr. Bowman was alone in the *Sixers* room when Amy arrived with her rewritten story.

"Mr. Bowman," she said, "I have something to tell you."

"Something *truthful* I hope," Mr. Bowman remarked pointedly.

Amy felt her face burn. "Yes," she said in a low voice. "The truth is that I lied."

"That story you wrote *was* pretty dramatic," Mr. Bowman said. "It might have gotten you first prize in a fiction-writing contest."

"I'm sorry," Amy said in an even lower voice. "I . . . I don't know why I did it. It wasn't honest." She handed him the story. "Elizabeth and I rewrote this last night. This time it's the truth."

Mr. Bowman scanned it quickly. "It *is* different," he agreed. "But even though it's not as dramatic, it's still a good story, and good reporting. It has all the essential facts—who, where, what, and when." He stopped. "But what about the *why*, Amy? You haven't included the cause of the fire."

Amy looked down. "That's because I don't know what it is—for sure, anyway. The insurance company won't give us their report until this afternoon."

Mr. Bowman laid Amy's story on his desk. "Well, there you are. You've got a perfect chance to make your reporting complete. We don't have to put the newspaper together until tomorrow. When you find out the cause of the fire, you can add it to your story."

"Yes, sir," Amy said unhappily. It seemed that no matter how hard she had tried, she couldn't escape having to tell the entire truth.

"What did Mr. Bowman say?" Elizabeth asked, as she and Amy walked home after school.

"He said we covered almost everything in our rewrite," Amy answered gloomily. "We've got the *who*, *what*, *when*, and *where*. All we need is the *why*."

"Oh, Amy," Elizabeth said in a sympathetic voice.

"Yeah, right." Amy kicked at a stone with her sneaker. "So tomorrow, I'll have to add the following sentence to the story. 'The fire was caused by Amy Sutton, who stupidly left a bag of hot ashes sitting on the carpet.' "

"But you don't *know* that yet," Elizabeth reminded her.

"I will in about three minutes," Amy replied as they came around the corner. "That's our car in your driveway. My mom's here. And I'll bet my dad's with her."

Mr. and Mrs. Sutton were sitting in the living

room, having a cup of coffee with Mrs. Wakefield.

"Hello, girls," Mrs. Wakefield said with a smile, as Elizabeth and Amy came into the room.

"We have some news for you, Amy." Mrs. Sutton put down her cup.

Amy's father gave a little laugh. "It's something you're probably not too anxious to hear."

Amy cast a stricken look at Elizabeth.

"We know that you've had a wonderful time here with the Wakefields," Mrs. Sutton went on. "But we've found a place for us to move into right away—this week, in fact."

"Our very own house?" she breathed.

Mr. Sutton nodded. "Our very own house." "Of course, we know you won't be pleased to hear that you're leaving the Wakefields' so soon. But you won't be going very far. Our new house is only a block away."

"A block away!" both girls squealed in unison.

"Oh, Dad, that's great!" Amy cried. "Just think, Elizabeth—only a block away! We can be together even *more* often!"

Mrs. Wakefield turned to Mrs. Sutton. "Have you gotten the insurance report yet, Dyan? Do they know what caused the fire?"

"Yes," Mrs. Sutton said. "We got it this afternoon."

Amy's smile faded away.

"I was really angry when I read the report," Mr. Sutton said.

Amy blindly turned toward the door, but Elizabeth caught her arm. "Wait," she whispered. "You can't go now, Amy."

"Angry?" Mrs. Wakefield asked.

"Yes," Mr. Sutton replied. "At myself. I knew the wiring in part of the house was old and worn-out. I should have had it replaced long ago."

"Wiring?" Amy asked in disbelief. "The fire was caused by bad wiring?"

Mr. Sutton nodded. "Believe me, we're going to get a full report on every inch of wire in our new house before we move in."

"See?" Elizabeth whispered. "It *wasn't* your fault after all!"

Amy gave an enormous sigh of relief. "I can't believe that everything's coming out OK," she said.

Her mother nodded. "Yes," she said, "the insurance company is paying for everything we lost." She smiled at Amy. "You see? Even tragic stories can have happy endings."

Happily, Elizabeth and Amy agreed.

"Did I leave anything out?" Amy asked Elizabeth. The girls were sitting on Jessica's bed. Amy had just told Jessica the entire true story.

"I don't think so," Elizabeth said.

Jessica stared at Amy. "You mean, you made it all up?"

"Not all of it, exactly," Amy said. "Just the

best parts. I'm sorry, Jessica. I didn't *mean* to lie to you, or to the others. But the truth is, I'm not a terrific heroine. I'm just somebody who forgets to tie her shoelaces."

Jessica laughed. "It's no big deal as far as I'm concerned," she said. "But I don't think I'd tell Lila, or Ellen either, if I were you. Just let it drop. They'll forget all about it in a few days."

'After the party, you mean," Elizabeth said.

"After the party," Jessica replied, "and after the jumping contest."

Elizabeth sat up straight. "The jumping contest?"

"Ellen just told me this evening," Jessica said. "There's a big contest at the fairgrounds. Ellen's decided that she's going to enter—and she's *determined* to win with that big white horse of hers."

Elizabeth smiled happily. "I think I'll go to Carson Stable right away and ask Ted Rogers to tell me what's going on!"

Will Ellen win the big competition? Find out in Sweet Valley Twins No. 45 **Lucy Takes the Reins.**

We hope you enjoyed reading this book. If you would like to receive further information about available titles in the Bantam series, just write to the address below, with your name and address: Kim Prior, Bantam Books, 61-63 Uxbridge Road, Ealing, London W5 5SA.

If you live in Australia or New Zealand and would like more information about the series, please write to:

Sally Porter
Transworld Publishers
(Australia) Pty Ltd
15-23 Helles Avenue
Moorebank
NSW 2170
AUSTRALIA

Kiri Martin
Transworld Publishers (NZ) Ltd
Cnr. Moselle and Waipareira
Avenues
Henderson
Auckland
NEW ZEALAND

All Bantam and Young Adult books are available at your bookshop or newsagent, or can be ordered at the following address: Corgi/Bantam Books, Cash Sales Department, PO Box 11, Falmouth, Cornwall, TR10 9EN.

Please list the title(s) you would like, and send together with a cheque or postal order. You should allow for the cost of book(s) plus postage and packing charges as follows:

80p for one book
£1.00 for two books
£1.20 for three books
£1.40 for four books
Five or more books free.

Please note that payment must be made in pounds sterling; other currencies are unacceptable.

(The above applies to readers in the UK and Republic of Ireland only)

BFPO customers, please allow for the cost of the book(s) plus the following for postage and packing: 80p for the first book, and 20p for each additional copy.

Overseas customers, please allow £1.50 for postage and packing for the first book, £1.00 for the second book, and 30p for each subsequent title ordered.

Created by Francine Pascal

Jessica and Elizabeth Wakefield have had lots of adventures in *Sweet Valley High* and *Sweet Valley Twins* . . .

Now read about the twins at age seven! All the fun that comes with being seven is part of *Sweet Valley Kids*. Read them all!

SWEET VALLEY HIGH

The top-selling teenage series starring identical twins Jessica and Elizabeth Wakefield and all their friends at Sweet Valley High. One new title every month!

SWEET VALLEY SUPER STARS

THE SADDLE CLUB

Bonnie Bryant

Share the thrills and spills of three girls drawn together by their special love of horses in this adventurous series.

1. HORSE CRAZY
2. HORSE SHY
3. HORSE SENSE
4. HORSE POWER
5. TRAIL MATES
6. DUDE RANCH
7. HORSE PLAY
8. HORSE SHOW
9. HOOF BEAT
10. RIDING CAMP
11. HORSE WISE
12. RODEO RIDER
13. STARLIGHT CHRISTMAS
14. SEA HORSE
15. TEAM PLAY